BOUNCER'S BOMBER

Gus Beaumont Thrillers
Book Four

Tony Rea

SAPERE
BOOKS

BOUNCER'S BOMBER

Published by Sapere Books.

24 Trafalgar Road, Ilkley, LS29 8HH

saperebooks.com

ISBN: 978-0-85495-679-1

Dedicated to the pilots and crews of the Free French Airforce 1940–45

ACKNOWLEDGEMENTS

My sincere thanks go to my wife Jane and to Patrick Rea for reading and critically commenting on early drafts of the text. Thanks also to everyone at the Ivybridge Writers' Group. Their wise observations and valuable comments have strengthened the story enormously, and any mistakes remain my own. As always, Amy Durant and the team at Sapere Books have contributed their experience and professionalism. Thank you all.

PART ONE: OCTOBER 1942

CHAPTER 1

There was nobody else in the Special Operations Executive library as Flight Lieutenant Gus Beaumont glanced at the large, wall-mounted clock. It was almost seven p.m. and Gus was wondering whether it was time to leave. He had a date with his fiancée, Eunice Hesketh, at eight and it would take him half an hour to walk from the SOE building on Baker Street to the RAF Club on Piccadilly, where they had agreed to meet.

Half an hour to kill.

The meet-up with Eunice was his main reason for making the journey down from RAF Tempsford to London. She had been spending a few days in the city, looking for bridal gown material and making all sorts of other arrangements for their wedding. Now that all of this was completed, Eunice was planning to travel up to Scotland, as she'd agreed to spend a couple of weeks with the parents of their friend, Duncan Farquhar.

It was a messy situation. Earlier in the year, in August, Duncan had been captured by the Germans near Dieppe. He was now a prisoner of war. However, Duncan had been wearing Gus's uniform when captured; therefore, his parents hadn't been officially notified of his capture. That had been for Gus and Eunice to explain, which they had done. Eunice was going to Scotland to fill them in on as much detail as possible, without giving away secret information about the Dieppe Raid and the circumstances of Duncan's capture.

Duncan's a POW for the second time in the war, thought Gus. *For heaven's sake, what an unpleasant achievement. What bloody bad luck.*

Gus had popped into 64 Baker Street to talk to Wing Commander Sir Alex Peacock about operational issues. However, he had found the wing commander absent; he had apparently phoned in sick that morning. The meeting had to be cancelled.

As the weather outside was wet and windy, Gus decided to spend the time in the small library which, alongside reference books and travel guides covering most of Europe, stocked a number of daily newspapers.

There wasn't a lot of news. A few days before, the Great War-era destroyer HMS *Veteran* had been torpedoed by a German submarine. It had sunk, all hands being lost. There was nothing about the Oslo Mosquito raid, but Gus had heard on the RAF grapevine that four Mosquito light bombers had attacked the headquarters of the Gestapo in Norway, in the hope this would boost the morale of the Norwegian people. It had failed, apparently. If that wasn't bad enough, the rumour was running wild that around eighty Norwegian civilians had been killed or injured and one of the bombers was lost. Bloody disaster — no wonder it wasn't in the papers. Was anything in this war going well for the Allies?

Gus heard the creaking of the library door. He glanced across the small room. There was now a second occupant of the library. Another member of Wing Commander Peacock's team had entered the room and was taking a pamphlet from one of the bookcases.

It was Squadron Leader Titus Grindlethorpe.

Earlier in the war, Grindlethorpe had commanded Gus in an operational army liaison squadron. The two had crossed swords a number of times and had a difficult working relationship. They were not on speaking terms these days, apart from what was necessary for work purposes.

Even so, Gus wondered whether he should say something, to show willing. In the event, it was Grindlethorpe who broke the silence.

"Nothing to do but read the bloody papers, Beaumont? Haven't you got work to do?" he said as he moved away from the bookcase, the pamphlet in his hand. He walked slowly towards a chair at the other end of the table, as far away from Gus as he could manage.

"I came to see Sir Alex, but he's off ill."

"Flu," said Grindlethorpe. "It's been going round. Lots of staff down with it."

"Well, I hope I don't catch it. I'm supposed to be flying tomorrow night."

"Yes, I know. Should be a straightforward sortie. This blasted wet weather is forecast to clear, so you shouldn't have any problems. Hope not, anyway. I'd hate to discover that you'd been shot down," said Grindlethorpe, chuckling in a sinister fashion. "Well, I've got work to do, even if you haven't. I've got this to read, then another few reports to sign off. I expect I'll be here until after nine. Then a nice fish supper and off home for a drink and a read. I do hope the operation goes well, Beaumont. We'd absolutely hate to lose you." He gave Gus an unpleasant smile, then lowered his eyes to the pamphlet and began reading.

When seven-thirty came, Gus left the library. Half an hour later, he met Eunice at the entrance to the RAF Club. They embraced, then he led her inside.

"What would you like to drink?" asked Gus. "Or shouldn't I ask?"

"You know what I'd like. A Kir Royale. But what have they got?"

"Two gin and tonics, please," said Gus to the bar tender.

"I suppose I'll have to make do," said Eunice.

"What time is your train?"

"Eleven. Plenty of time. Can we get something to eat here?"

"Yes, they'll have something."

"It's a bit late, sir," said an orderly, overhearing them. He was an elderly chap, probably a Great War veteran, thought Gus. "But I'm sure we can rustle up something, even if it's just a sandwich. Leave it with me."

Gus took the two glasses and led Eunice to a table.

"Hope they've got more than a bloody sandwich," she said. "I'm famished."

"Did you find the right material? For the wedding dress?"

"Yes. But the less you know, the better. We don't want to tempt fate, do we? It's traditional. The dress will be white, but that's all I'm going to say about it, Gus. So don't ask anything more."

"I won't. You look tired, Eunice. Will you sleep on the journey?"

"I'll try. But if not, I'm reading this." Eunice pulled a book from her handbag and thrust it towards him. As he took hold of the book, Gus noticed the engagement ring on the third finger of her left hand and, not for the first time, marvelled at how well it suited his fiancée. It had been his late mother's, purchased by his father just after the end of the Great War. It must have been one of the first of its type, as it featured the new baguette cut gemstones which came from France.

This one was stunning. The central emerald was bordered by two diamonds which sparkled in the light of a table lamp. The stones were set in a flat-profile band of the purest platinum, which had rounded sides. It was said that only those women who saw themselves as different and daring were drawn to this cut of stone, and this was true of both Gus's mother, Magda

Beaumont, and Eunice. Magda and his fiancée had always liked each other, and Eunice had been delighted when Gus had proposed to her and offered the ring.

He glanced at the book. "*The Sittaford Mystery*? Agatha Christie? Not your usual thing, is it?"

"Oh don't be such a snob; there's a time and place for everything. Nothing wrong with a light read on a long train journey. Anyway, I've started it and it's quite good."

The orderly arrived with food: a plate of pie and mash for each of them. "Steak and kidney, sir and miss. I hope that will be acceptable?"

"Lovely," said Eunice.

"Please could you bring us some more drinks? I'll have a pint of beer. Eunice?"

"A small glass of water, please."

"Straight away, miss."

After they had finished eating, the conversation turned back to their forthcoming wedding. It was planned for early next year.

They'd decided to have a simple church service in central London with their wedding breakfast reception here at the RAF Club. The guestlist was fairly well advanced, if not fixed. Gus's cousin, Staś Rosen, would be best man. Other Poles, including Butch Paderewski, would be there together with friends from some of the other units Gus had served with. Eunice's friends Grace and Cathy would be there, of course. With both her parents killed in the London Bombing, Eunice's uncle, Herbert, was to give her away.

"Did we get any response from Milly Turner?"

"Not so far," replied Eunice. "I do hope she's all right." Their friend Milly had been with the Women's Auxiliary Air Force at the beginning of the war, during which time she had met and fallen in love with fighter pilot Tunio Nowacki, another friend of theirs. When Milly had discovered she was pregnant, they had planned to marry, but before they could do so Tunio had been killed by a Nazi pilot.

"What about Baudouin and Claude?" Gus asked, referring to the two French Resistance fighters who had escaped from Dieppe with Eunice.

"They'll be there, so long as they're not posted away."

"Of course. That goes for almost everyone," said Gus.

"Yes. Are you all right, dear?"

"Me? Yes, I'm fine. Why do you ask?"

"Well, you thought I looked tired. But compared to you... It's just that you look so worn-out all of a sudden. You've even got bags under your eyes."

"Gosh, you really know how to compliment a man."

"Sorry, I didn't mean to sound rude."

"You're probably right. I've been having a bit of trouble sleeping, as it happens. Maybe it's catching up with me. But I'm fine, Eunice, honest."

"Are you fit to fly?"

"Of course I'm fit to fly. Stop worrying. I'm due to go off tomorrow night, as it happens. Eunice, don't burden yourself fretting about me. Look, it's almost time we were off."

"Is it still raining outside?"

"Expect so, but it's supposed to clear later. We'll get a cab to King's Cross, shall we?"

"Yes," said Eunice, with a smile. "That will be best."

At King's Cross station, Gus and Eunice hugged and kissed farewell. She pushed a key into his hand. "Make sure you lock up tomorrow morning, and don't leave any lights on, will you? I know what you're like. Mr Forgetful."

"Don't worry. And remember to give my best wishes to Mr and Mrs Farquhar. I still feel bad about leaving Duncan in France."

"Gus, it's not your fault. Now, off you go and get a good night's sleep."

"Yes," he said, though he thought it would be a miracle if he did.

CHAPTER 2

"Two eggs you asked for, wasn't it, Mr Beaumont, sir? Both with soft yolks?" asked Flight Sergeant Booker.

"That's right, Bill," said Gus, gazing eagerly at the mixed grill supper that Booker placed on the table in front of him.

"And the steak, I've kept just a little bit pink in the middle," said Sergeant Booker, "as usual, sir."

"Champion, Bill," said Gus. "Thanks."

Bill Booker was one of the two sergeants based at the cottage on the Special Operations Executive's outpost at RAF Tangmere, near Chichester. They acted as minders, looking after the SOE pilots. This included providing meals before and after each sortie, and Bill was an excellent cook.

The Lysander Flight of the SOE's 161 (Special Duties) Squadron, which Gus was serving with, was actually based at RAF Tempsford, in the East Midlands. Tangmere was used as the operational departure point to give the Lizzies a slightly longer range.

"I'll fetch you another cuppa — just milk, isn't it? No sugar?"

"That's the ticket, Bill. Just a drop of milk."

Gus tucked into the pre-flight supper. A small steak, medium rare. A lamb chop, also pinkish. Two sausages, half a tomato, a large field mushroom and two eggs with soft yolks.

Summer was definitely over, and the weather had begun to turn cold. Gus wore a roll-necked, woollen sweater under the grey, tailored jacket of his uniform. He wore his leather flying jacket over this, which was covered with the braids of a Flight Lieutenant, and on top of this went his Mae West.

Thirty minutes later, his flying helmet and parachute in hand, Gus walked out into the darkness to the aeroplane standing at the side of the taxiway, close to the cottage. The Westland Lysander was a high-winged monoplane designed for close support of the army, and that was where his RAF career had begun.

Gus had plenty of experience with Lizzies, having first flown one over France in 1940. He liked them. They were easy to handle, almost impossible to stall and provided the crew with excellent views downwards on both sides. The Lysanders belonging to 161 Squadron, however, bore little resemblance to the standard version flown by Gus at the beginning of the war. They had been modified for their new, secretive role. The underneath was painted matt black to help conceal it from searchlights. Gone was the rear gunner's equipment, and the rear cockpit could accommodate three or four Joes — agents. A ladder was fixed to the port side so that the Joes, or occasionally escapees, could clamber in and out more easily. Lastly, a gigantic, torpedo-shaped, one-hundred-and-fifty-gallon petrol tank was slung under the fuselage, giving the Lizzies an enormous range of over one thousand miles.

Gus looked up at the full moon which cast its milky light over Tangmere, then he clambered up into the cockpit and, like clockwork, went through the checks. After many Lysander flights, these checks were becoming mechanical, instinctive. All the more reason for a double-check. His hand felt for the tail trim wheel. Good, it was fully forward in the take-off position.

There was just one Joe to take out tonight. A middle-aged man, who now scaled the ladder fixed to the side of the Lysander. Gus wondered if he knew Eunice, also an SOE agent. He dared not ask, for SOE pilots knowing their passengers was severely frowned upon.

"You've got more space than usual," he shouted over his shoulder, "so strap yourself in and relax! There's a flask of hot chocolate and some biscuits. All we could manage, I'm afraid."

The Joe smiled eagerly. "Thanks, I'm ravenous!"

"Well, help yourself once we're up. Otherwise, sit back and enjoy the flight."

With the brakes on hard, Gus pushed forward on the throttle lever with his left hand to open up the powerful Bristol Mercury engine of the Lysander, and when it was almost up to maximum prop speed he let off the brakes. The Lysander was airborne within yards and heading due east, into wind. Once at altitude, Gus got on course for a spot on the French coast that was known for the absence of German flak.

They crossed the Channel. Gus altered course to clear Le Mans and then head directly towards the landing zone, which was south of the river Loire. He shouted back to the Joe again, "I fancy a cup of chocolate! Could you do the honours?"

"All right," answered the Joe, fidgeting around. He soon produced a cup of steaming liquid. "Here you are. I've scoffed most of the biscuits, but there are one or two left. Want one?"

"Yes, please. Always helps, I find. Help yourself to the last one, if you like."

"Thanks, I will. I say, have you done much of this sort of thing?" the Joe asked. "No complaints, you understand. You seem sound enough."

"Now, there's a compliment," said Gus with a smile. "Thanks. Nice to know you think I'm up to it, but you've not seen me land yet."

"Sorry, I just meant…"

"It's all right, only joking. You're allowed to ask."

"So, have you been around these planes for a while?"

"I've done quite a bit, I suppose. About a dozen moonlight sorties in Lysanders. One or two in the Lockheed Hudson twin-engined kites."

"But you've always been on transport types?"

"This is a bit more than a transport run."

"What I'm getting at is, you've not been flying fighters or bombers?"

In fact, Gus had flown fighters — Hurricanes in the Battle of Britain, and Blenheim bombers in Greece.

"I flew Lysanders at the beginning of the war," he said. "In fact, I may have been the first pilot to attack the Jerries in anger. Certainly from a Lizzie."

"Really?"

"Yes. I was on a recce run back in May 1940 and we spotted Jerry armour coming out of some woods. I rather lost my head and had a go at them. Regular Lysanders are fitted with a couple of Brownings."

"Really? Where on earth do they fix those?"

"On the undercarriage. There are stub-wings — you probably didn't notice. The machine guns go there."

"And did you hit anything? Or shouldn't I ask?"

"You have asked, and yes, I did, as a matter of fact. Got at least one of those BMW armed motorbike and sidecar jobs. Maybe two. Then I was chased off by a Bf-109. Lost my rear gunner, though. I was reprimanded for it by a pompous old squadron leader back at base."

"Well, good for you — you showed your mettle! What did you do afterwards?"

"I was posted to other squadrons, flying all sorts of kites. Blighty, Greece, Malta. Been with this outfit since last spring."

The chatter petered out, and Gus focused on his navigation. He had cut numerous strips from a 1:500,000 map; each strip had his planned route in the middle and around fifty miles on each side. He had taped together the strips to make a single linear map, which he then carefully folded so that he could hold it in one hand and study it whilst flying. He looked at it now. On course. Good. He also had his 'gen' cards. These held navigational data for each leg of the trip and were taped onto the blank part of the linear route map, which showed nothing but English Channel.

Gus looked down at the moonlit countryside, the river Loire snaking through it. He checked the compass and altered course slightly to take him towards the target zone. "Not long now," he muttered as he switched his attention to a 1:250,000 map which gave much more detail of the landing zone.

After a few minutes, Gus saw the landing zone.

"There it is!" he called to the Joe. "See? That regular, flashing white light down there?"

The man gazed out into the darkness.

"See it? Dot dot dot dash, dot dot, dash dot dash dot. Vic. That's our codeword. I expect the French down there can hear the Lysander's engine."

"I hope they are French," said the Joe, "and not..."

"Don't worry."

Gus steered the plane towards the flashing light. Using the underwing light, he signalled the corresponding letter. Dot dot dash dot. F.

The instant he did so, the flashing from the ground ceased and new lights were lit. Flares that burned orange, tinged with white. These new lights marked out a letter L. A solitary light marked the top end of the longer side, which Gus knew would be about a hundred and fifty yards. More than enough for the Lysander. Two more flares, closer together, marked the shorter edge of the 'L' shape and the end of usable landing room. This was the makeshift landing strip Gus was aiming for.

He was approaching downwind, so Gus overshot the strip, turned and put the Lysander onto a new approach. He was now heading towards the two flares marking the shorter edge, flying parallel with the longer side of the L. So long as the agents on the ground had done their work well, this would head Gus into whatever wind there was down there.

As Gus slowed the aircraft, the automatic wing slats and slotted flaps adjusted to prevent the Lysander stalling. He touched down midway along the strip towards the two flares which marked the bottom of the inverted letter L. Gus turned around between the two flares, taxied back to the opposite end of the strip and turned again. As he set the tail trim wheel for take-off, a figure came running out of the woods on the port side of the Lysander.

"Here's our reception committee," he said to his passenger, who was already unstrapping and getting himself ready to vacate the Lizzie.

"Thanks!" he shouted as he clambered down the ladder.

"Good luck!" Gus shouted back, over the noise of the engine as the Joe ran away towards the dark figures on the ground.

Through the darkness, Gus could make out a car. Two people quickly got out of it and came around the rear of the Lysander, making for the port side. A man clambered up the Lysander's ladder. Once at the top, he turned and beckoned to the other person. Two small suitcases were passed up to him. Then a woman climbed up the ladder and into the cockpit.

"Ready?" asked Gus.

"Ready," replied the man.

"Then strap yourselves in. We're off."

Gus waved to the figure on the ground. With the brakes on hard, he pushed forward on the throttle lever with his left hand to open up the engine. Noise and vibration flooded the cockpit. Once it was almost up to maximum prop speed, Gus checked the tail trim wheel again, then let off the brakes. The Lysander rushed along the grassy strip and was airborne within yards. Gus flew upwards, wanting to reach the desired altitude, and headed north, towards Le Mans. As they gained height and the temperature dropped, condensation began to form on the inside of the Lysander's Perspex cockpit canopy. Gus noticed the man trying to clean away the vapour, so that he might search downwards for a glimpse of where they were.

"Sit back and try to relax," he said to his passengers.

"Relax?" said the man. "I should be so lucky."

CHAPTER 3

Everything seemed to happen at once.

"Look out!" cried the woman. "There's something out there. A plane, to our left. Here it comes!"

Gus had no time to look left. Instinctively, he rolled the Lysander violently to starboard, away from whatever the imminent threat was. Simultaneously, he throttled off, for experience had taught him one valuable lesson: the best way to dodge anything in a Lizzie was to decelerate, for nothing could match a Lysander for slowness.

As Gus made these automatic, almost involuntary moves to avoid the danger, bullets ripped into the side of the Lysander, some of them ricocheting around. Part of the Perspex canopy on the port side of the rear cockpit shattered, with hundreds of sharp shards sent flying around the cockpit. Gus saw blood splattered onto the opposite side of the canopy. He had no idea whose blood it was and had no time to investigate as he felt the vibrations of more machine-gun bullets ripping into the Lysander, shaking it violently.

Up until this point, Gus had acted instinctively. Now, perhaps just fifteen seconds after the woman's screams and his first avoiding action, his training in the RAF procedure to avoid night fighters or escape a searchlight beam kicked in.

"Hold on!" he shouted as he began to put the aeroplane into a corkscrew manoeuvre, downwards and away from danger. Quick to respond to his finesse at the controls, the Lysander began to spiral to the ground. Glancing up and ahead, Gus glimpsed the looming shape of a twin-engined aeroplane speeding away from him.

"He'll come back for us!" screamed the man behind Gus. "We're bloody well done for!"

Quickly, Gus looked again, scanning the sky for a clue as to what might be happening. He thought he caught sight of the dim red glow of the night fighter's exhausts disappearing into the darkness.

"I doubt it," said Gus, hoping he was right, and pulling the Lysander out of its spiralling dive. "He's long gone and well away by now. Are either of you injured?"

"I'm fine," said the woman. "Just banged my arm. It hurts a little, but nothing broken. Bit of a cut. He's bleeding — head wound."

"I didn't feel anything," said the man. "I wasn't hit by a bullet. At least I don't think so. My head's bloody throbbing now, though."

"Hit by Perspex. Or a ricochet, perhaps," offered Gus. "Can you patch him up with something? Cover your own wound, too."

"Yes, I'll use my scarf. Don't worry," the woman added for her companion's sake, "it's clean."

"What about radar?" asked the man nervously, regaining his senses if not his composure. "Surely the Jerries will still be tracking us?"

"I don't think so. I don't think that fighter was directed to us; it most probably came upon us by accident."

"How do you know?"

"We're well away from any German ground-based radar stations. Maybe his on-board radar found us, maybe not. Either way, I'm confident he's gone now," lied Gus, "so don't worry."

He knew very well that the German night fighters were now equipped with airborne radar, which was effective up to just over two miles and could bring the fighter back to within seven hundred feet of them. But there was no point burdening his passengers with this. Anyway, he thought it unlikely.

"Look," he said, "I need to do an instrument check. Be quiet for a moment, would you?"

With the Lysander flying level now, and beginning to gain height with a view to getting back on course, Gus scanned his flying instruments. Things seemed undamaged, but when he looked down at the compass, he saw it was shattered. A stray bullet from the night fighter must have knocked it out. Where was he? He looked around for the moon. *I'll never fly again without taking a handheld compass*, he thought. He looked down. Nothing but darkness. He strained. Was that the French coast he could see off in the distance? He headed for it, hoping so.

"Anything damaged back there? Any holes in the fuselage?" he asked his passengers.

"I don't think so, apart from the cockpit cover. All the left-hand side of it is gone. But nothing else obvious, anyhow."

"That's good."

"What was it, the plane that attacked us?" asked the woman.

"Difficult to be sure. It was twin-engined, but all of the Jerry night fighters are. Maybe a Messerschmitt Bf-110, or a Junkers Ju-88, perhaps. We'll never know. I just can't think what it was doing out here. We're miles away from any of our Bomber routes; they all fly in over Belgium and Holland. Possibly he was out training. I don't know."

"He was armed."

He was indeed, thought Gus. "Bit of bad news, I'm afraid," he said. "Compass isn't working. We're a tad lost."

"What do you mean, a tad lost?" asked the man, angrily.

"Properly lost, if you prefer. We're still over France. I think I can see the coast, but I don't know for sure which bit of coast it is."

He squinted, but all he could make out ahead of them was a long, indeterminate line where land met water. He brought the Lysander down to gain a better view of the ground as he hunted for identifiable landmarks. It was no use; everything looked fuzzy. He couldn't make out what part of the coast they were about to cross. Was he in the flak-free gap?

As if to answer him, a sudden burst of anti-aircraft fire exploded on the right-hand side of the Lysander. The aeroplane jolted violently.

"Hang on!" cried Gus, and he put the Lizzie into another corkscrewing dive. Another explosion rocked them. Then a third. Searchlights beamed upwards but, thankfully, failed to pick them out and hold them in its powerful beam. There was a fourth blast, but by now the explosions were well above them.

The man cursed. "We're doomed!"

Then there was silence and calm. Miraculously, the ack-ack fire had stopped. Gus was able to level off and once again climb upwards, high into the night sky. A second instrument check told Gus that the fuel level had gone down alarmingly since the last time he'd looked at it, just after the night fighter attack. The tank must have been holed either by a bullet or shrapnel from the flak, he thought. *Don't tell them. Don't let on.*

Gus scanned both sky and surface again. His original planned route was to fly over the Cotentin peninsula. Get to the northern end of that, fly due north and he'd hit Southampton or Bournemouth. But he didn't know where he was and had no compass to guide him. He scanned the sky in search of the Pole Star, but light cloud cover had developed.

He could see little of anything. Certainly there was no Pole Star to be seen.

The French coast was behind them now, Gus was sure of it. That was where the anti-aircraft fire had come from. It had to be. If he could just keep on a northerly course, then he would eventually reach somewhere in England. The prevailing wind was a westerly. That would have to serve him as a compass. It was his only hope. He knew he must keep to port in order to allow for leeway. But how far to port should he steer? It was impossible to know for certain.

"I'm going to go into the wind a bit, then just keep everything on a steady course until we're over England. Once we get there, I'll need you to keep a good lookout for me, if you will."

"How long will it take?"

"The English coast should be…"

"Should be?" shouted the man.

"Oh, do shut up," said the woman.

"The English coast is about seventy miles away," said Gus, in the most confident tone he could muster, hoping it was true. If not, they might run out of petrol. He glanced at the speedometer, reduced his speed a little to conserve fuel and did some mental arithmetic.

"We're now flying at a hundred and forty miles per hour, so half an hour," said Gus, praying that there was enough fuel to get them to safety. "There's some cocoa in the flask if you fancy a sip, but all the biscuits are gone. Sorry about that."

The man remained silent and surly. "I don't think I want anything at the moment, thank you," said the woman.

After thirty minutes, when they ought to have been over southern England, there was nothing but sea below them. Gus reduced height to give himself a better view. There was no land to be seen.

Ten minutes later, he spotted what could be a coastline.

"Look down there — is that land?"

"Could be," said the woman.

Five minutes later, she shouted, "Down there, to the right!"

Gus glanced down. At last, they were flying over a land mass.

"Looks like an airfield," said Gus. "Strap in tight. That machine-gun burst from the night fighter might well have punctured a tyre. Both, if we're very unlucky."

He steered the Lysander downwind of the strip, then turned to approach into the wind. Gus brought the Lizzie in, the altitude dial showing height above ground level: five hundred feet, four hundred and fifty feet, four hundred feet. Flaps down. He saw the runway clearly now, but the start of it was a good two hundred yards away in the distance. Bugger! Gus opened the throttle, increased speed and pulled the aircraft up into the black sky.

"What the bloody hell are you doing?" yelled the man from the rear of the cockpit.

"Sorry. Mistimed it. We'll go around and have another bash."

He circled and approached the base again, watching the instruments. As he did so, the engine stuttered and came to a stop.

"What's going on?" shouted the man.

"Calm down. We're out of fuel, that's all."

"Out of fuel? You're bloody incompetent, man!"

"That fighter must have got the petrol tanks as well as the compass. Don't worry — we can glide in. Safer that way, anyhow. Nothing to catch fire if we crash-land."

"Oh my God!" wailed the man.

One eye constantly on the altitude dial, Gus brought the Lysander down. Two hundred feet, one hundred and fifty, one hundred, fifty feet.

Thump! Up the Lysander went, the wings tilting severely. Then down again, with a thud.

Relieved that all the tyres seemed to be intact, Gus taxied to the buildings he could see in the middle distance. As he stopped the Lysander, a group of men came out to meet them, gazing at the unfamiliar aeroplane.

"Where am I?" Gus shouted down to an airman wearing NCO stripes.

"RAF Davidstow Moor, sir."

"Put a guard around the kite!" barked Gus. "Nobody is to go anywhere near it. Understand?"

"Yes, sir."

Gus unstrapped and turned to speak to the two Joes in the rear of this cockpit. "You two stay put," he said. "I'll find out what I can and work out how to get us home."

Gus climbed out of the cockpit and shimmied down the ladder.

"Davidstow Moor? Coastal Command base in Cornwall, yes?" he said to the airman.

"That's right, sir. Where have you come from?"

"Never mind that. Take me to your intelligence officer, at the double."

CHAPTER 4

Gus was quickly introduced to Pilot Officer Billy Balsdon, the intelligence officer at RAF Davidstow Moor, and now stood before him in a small office.

"I'm Gus Beaumont, from 161 Squadron. Can't tell you too much, I'm afraid. Bit hush-hush. Suffice to say I have two important and very secret passengers in the kite and all three of us need a feed and a bit of kip. Oh, and I need your lads to give the Lizzie the once-over. She was losing fuel, and the compass is shot up."

"The officers' mess will be open for breakfast soon. The three of you can eat there."

"I can, but not them. They need a bit of privacy. The fewer of your staff who know they're here, the better."

"I'll have to tell the Station Commander."

"Naturally."

"There's a couple of spare rooms over near the squash court. I suppose they could be billeted there. We can take some food to them. But how to get them there without them being seen?"

"You've an ambulance on base?"

"Of course."

"Get that to drive up close to the Lizzie. You and I can supervise the passengers into the ambulance, and it can take them to their billets. Near the squash court, you said?"

"Yes. Do you play?"

"A bit. Not very good. More of a rugby man, to be honest."

"Fancy a game before you go? I'll fix you up with some kit and a racquet, if you like."

"Well, I... Look, can we talk about that later?"

"Sure."

"Come on, then. Let's get this done."

The ambulance was a converted Austin 30cwt lorry exactly like those Gus had seen on just about every RAF base he'd been to. It was grey, with a red cross inside a white roundel painted on each side. A burly sergeant was in the driver's seat, and Billy sat beside him.

Gus got into the back. It was larger inside than he'd imagined, with room for four stretcher cases and associated medics. Gus sat on the hard wooden seat as the ambulance drove off. Soon the ambulance came to a lurching halt and Gus listened to the orders being barked at the airmen by the sergeant.

"Right, you men!" he shouted to the four airmen on guard. "I want one of you on each wingtip, one at the front of the kite and the other at the back. You're all to face outwards, away from the plane, and keep a good watch for anyone loitering and gawping at it. Got that?"

"Yes, Sergeant!"

"C'mon," shouted the sergeant, playing a good game, "out with them stretchers! Be quick about it!"

Gus and Billy led the two Joes into the darkness of the ambulance, both staying in the back this time as the sergeant drove away.

"Where are we going?" asked the man.

"Pilot Officer Balsdon has found you billets," said Gus.

"Don't worry. Got you rooms to yourselves," said Billy.

"Private bathroom?"

"For the lady," said Billy. "You'll have to use the squash court changing rooms."

The man frowned.

"Alternatively, just don't bother to wash," added Gus.

The ambulance stopped at the squash courts and the Joes got out. Billy showed them to their accommodation then came back to join Gus. They drove off, giving the agents time to settle themselves.

"Don't worry about him," said Gus. "He's got a bit of a cut on his head. Bled a lot in the plane, but it can't be anything too serious."

"I'll have the medical officer look him over, just in case."

A couple of hours later, as the weak, early autumn sun began to rise, Gus and Billy went over to the accommodation with trays of food and drink.

"The MO says he's fine," said Billy as he knocked on the male Joe's door. "The bleeding's stopped, so I might invite him for a game of squash later. If he plays."

"You seem to be a bit obsessed with squash, if you don't mind me saying."

"Totally. Gave me my name in the mess, as a matter of fact."

"Which is?"

"Squashed Balls," smiled Billy. "Some ruddy rude chaps in RAF messes these days, don't you know! You have a nickname?"

"Bouncer."

"Bouncer? Why's that?"

"Some heavy landings in the early days."

"Ah, I see," said Billy with a smile. "Yes. You were a bit heavy-handed landing the Lizzie earlier, I noticed, Bouncer."

"Shall we get on with this?"

Gus left Billy and walked towards the room where the woman had been billeted. He knocked on the door, and she called out, "Yes? Who is it?"

"It's me. The Lysander pilot. Got some tucker if you're hungry."

She opened the door. "Come on in."

Gus went in and placed the tray on a small desk close to the one window.

"Can't vouch for the food and drink, I'm afraid. Not my base. Well, I suppose you must have worked that out."

"I wanted to thank you," she said.

"Thank me?"

"For getting us out of that pickle."

"You shouldn't thank me. I made mistakes up there. Poor navigating. Then I made a mess of the landing approach. I should have done better."

"We all make mistakes, and anyway, I didn't notice," she replied. "Stay a while, can you?"

"A short while, yes."

"Have a seat."

Gus took the one chair in the room, by the desk. The woman perched on the end of the bed. She was petite and had shoulder-length, fair hair. Perhaps unsurprisingly, she was dressed in a tight-fitting, French style frock. She reminded Gus of Eunice, though not as tall.

"Last night I thought we were going to be shot out of the bloody sky," she said. "You acted so quickly."

"The Jerry pilot made a mistake, as well. He opened fire from too far away. If he'd have kept his nerve and got closer, then we would have been shot out of the sky. It was only some of his machine-gun bullets that hit us. If he had cannons, then those shells missed us completely. It was sheer chance. Bad luck that he came across us at all, and our good fortune he made a hash of it. Bad luck the ack-ack gunners spotted us later; a blessing their fire did little or no damage. Bad luck the

34

petrol tank was holed, a godsend we didn't catch fire up there, or have the fuel run out on us over the sea. Oh, and bad luck that my compass got damaged. I don't think it will mend."

The woman offered him her hand. "I'm Susan," she said. Gus knew enough not to quiz her any further. She may indeed be Susan, but then again she might not be. In all probability she was lying to cover herself. Anyway, only yesterday she would have been somebody else: Camille, or Jean, or Clarice.

"Gus Beaumont," he said, "Bouncer in the mess, and to friends."

"Thanks again, Bouncer," she said. "I still say you kept your cool and did a pretty good job."

"Thanks," he replied, embarrassed. "Your colleague, there — he seems a bit jumpy."

"I agree. He's a bit of a misery, too. I don't know him. Only met him last night, in the car going to the pick-up. That's what it's like, you know."

"Yes, I know. Look," Gus said, getting up, "I need to get back to the kite and see how the riggers and engineers are getting along. You tuck in to your breakfast and I'll pop back later, let you know the lie of the land."

"Please go ahead," she said, raising the coffee cup to her lips. "Don't you worry about me."

CHAPTER 5

The following morning, Gus went over to the Lysander to get
a debrief on the damage, hoping for good news. He sought out
the NCO leading the ground crew charged with the task of
getting the aeroplane airworthy again. The NCO gave him a
comprehensive rundown of the job in hand.

"We've patched up the petrol tanks, sir — both of them
were holed. They'll be all right for now, but I'd get your own
chaps to inspect again once you're back on base."

"Yes, I'll do that."

"We don't have a suitable compass to replace the ruined one
—"

"I won't need a compass to take her home in daylight," Gus
interrupted.

"But there's worse news, sir. The tailplane is pretty badly
shot up, including the inner workings. We can't get it to move
from the position it's stuck in."

"You're telling me that you can't move the tailplane into the
take-off position?"

Gus knew that a badly trimmed tailplane could be disastrous
for a Lysander. If it was positioned incorrectly, there was no
way of countering it once the aeroplane was powering along a
runway. It wouldn't leave the ground, resulting in a crash.

"That's right, sir."

"Can't you mend it?"

"We can, sir. But it'll take a few days to get the bits and bobs
we need, and when we do get the spares, well —" the NCO
pointed to an array of aeroplanes on the apron — "we've got

all these to service too, sir. I'm afraid you're grounded for a while. Sorry we can't be more helpful."

Gus looked at the aircraft in front of them. RAF Davidstow Moor was a coastal command base and held an array of different aircraft. Around the perimeter there were Bristol Beaufighters, Lockheed Hudsons and two Vickers Warwicks, a version of the Wellington bomber fitted out for maritime reconnaissance. Near the control tower was a Supermarine Walrus, a single-engined, biplane flying boat used for air sea rescue. These engineers and riggers had their work cut out and, what's more, had probably never worked on a Lysander in their careers. Perhaps he would have time for a game of squash with Billy 'Squashed Balls' Balsdon after all.

"It's all right, Sergeant. Not your fault at all."

No, not his fault. Nobody's fault but his own.

Later in the morning, Gus made a telephone call to Tempsford, relaying the news. Then he met up with the two Joes, informing them of the situation.

"What are we going to do?" demanded the male agent.

"Squadron will send someone down for you tomorrow. Take you back to Tangmere for debrief," said Gus.

"What about you?" asked Susan.

"I have to wait here until the Lysander's fixed."

"So, the three of us are here tonight," she said.

"Correct."

"Why don't we go out for a drink or something then?"

"Good idea," said Gus.

"We can't possibly," said the man.

"Why can't we?" demanded Susan, arms folded across her chest.

"Nobody has suggested we're confined to barracks," said Gus. "I'm sure we'll be able to borrow a car from someone."

"Well, not for me," said the man. "I'd rather have another game of squash against that pilot officer. He bloody well beat me this morning. I'm not having that!"

"Each to his own," said Susan, winking at Gus.

Camelford was the closest town to RAF Davidstow. Gus wangled the loan of a black Humber Sprite saloon from Billy and, at half past six that evening, he drove himself and Susan along the five miles of winding, pitch-black lane that led to the town. When they got there, they realised that 'town' was an exaggeration.

Gus parked the car on the main street and turned off the ignition. They looked around the deserted street.

"Do you know," said Gus, "until 1932, Camelford returned two members of Parliament to Westminster?"

"Really? But there's not a lot here now. It seems almost uninhabited. Anyway, how do you know that?"

"Studied history before the war. I don't think there was much around in those days either. It was one of what were known as *rotten boroughs*. The seats in Parliament were obtained by bribes."

They got out of the car and found the local pub, the Masons Arms.

"What would you like to drink, Susan?" Gus asked as they went inside.

"No. Let me. It was my idea to come," she replied. Gus looked askance at her. "Don't give me that look. You might find it a bit unusual, but women can order at a bar, you know! And pay! It's a bit easier in France. You know, with their Republican traditions. '*Liberté, égalité, fraternité*' and all that. But even there, it's still a bit out of the ordinary. What will you have, Bouncer?"

"A pint of bitter, please."

"A pint of bitter and a gin and tonic, please," she said to the barman.

They took their drinks to a table and sat down.

"Cheers," said Gus.

"Cheers. I always fancied being a pilot."

"Really?"

"Yes, but it's another thing that's not so easy for women to do."

"I knew a woman who was an Air Transport Auxiliary pilot, actually," said Gus.

"Really? What's she called?"

"Bunty. Bunty Kermode."

"Girlfriend? If you don't mind me asking?"

"Well, sort of. Yes."

"And you say you knew her? What happened? Did it finish?"

"She was killed — in a tip-and-run raid earlier this year. Blasted Focke-Wulf 190 fighter bomber."

"I'm sorry."

"Well, these things happen. There is a war on, you know?"

"So you're a ... what is it? A free agent these days?"

"No. Actually, I'm engaged to be married."

"Oh, a quick worker!"

"It was all a bit complicated, back then."

"Sorry, Bouncer. I didn't realise. Anyway, perhaps men should wear engagement rings like women do. It would make things a darn sight easier, wouldn't it?"

"I suppose so, yes."

"What's she called? Your fiancée?"

"Eunice."

"And what does she do?"

"She's in your line of work, actually."

"An agent? SOE?"

"Yes."

"You're not supposed to know."

"I know. But I do. It's complicated, as I said. Anyway, all that will have to stop once we're married. She'll be busy having babies and keeping home." He laughed.

"And Eunice knows this, does she? You've discussed everything?"

"Well ... we..."

"Thought as much. You haven't talked about it, have you? She might feel differently, you know? There's a war on, as you said, and she might feel she has a part to play in it. A duty, even."

"Is that how you feel?"

"Yes, it is, as a matter of fact." Susan looked at the clock. "It's time we got back. Please may I drive the car this time?"

Gus hesitated.

"You really do have a lot to learn, Bouncer," she said. "You make all sorts of assumptions about women, don't you?"

Later that night, as he lay in bed, Gus reviewed the conversation he'd had with Susan. He had assumed too much. Yes, that was what it was. Why had he supposed that Susan couldn't drive a car or would prefer to have a man drive her around? It was also his assumption, nothing more, that Eunice would stay at the house he had inherited in Winchester once they were married, whilst he carried on in the RAF until the end of the war.

Susan was right; Eunice might have other ideas. They hadn't discussed it. Everything had happened in such a whirlwind. He'd never thought for a moment that Eunice would want to go back to France, with all the dangers it entailed.

For now, Eunice was on leave. The rest would do her good, after all the stress she'd been through in Dieppe. Now he was tired. It was time to put thoughts of Eunice out of his mind, time to concentrate on sleep.

CHAPTER 6

Early the following morning, Gus called on Susan with a breakfast tray.

"Can I ask you for some advice?" he said, as she munched on a bacon sandwich.

"Of course."

"It's about what we were discussing last night. About Eunice, my fiancée and, well, how we might organise things once we're married."

"Yes?"

"Well, what do you think I should do?"

"I think you need to talk to her about it. Write to her, in the first instance, if you'd prefer. Especially if you're not going to see her for a while. But don't leave it. If it turns out you both want the same thing, then it's easy."

"And if we don't?"

"Then you need to compromise. One of you simply giving in to the other won't work. Not in the long run."

Gus looked worried.

Susan smiled. "Just talk to her. I don't suppose your conversation will throw up anything you can't handle. If it does, then sorry to be blunt, but it might mean you're simply not suited to one other."

"I hope you're wrong about that," said Gus. "Come on, we'd better get ourselves outside and ready. Your air-taxi won't be long now."

Outside they heard an engine sound in the east. They scanned the sky, then Gus pointed as an aeroplane emerged from the cloud cover.

"This is it," he said, recognising the familiar sound and sight of a Lysander. It was the Lizzie sent down from Tempsford, as promised, to pick up Susan and the other Joe.

As the aeroplane taxied towards the control tower, Gus saw that his friend Jack 'Doggie' Russell was the pilot, waving his pipe and smiling a cheery hello from the cockpit.

"You're in safe hands," he said to Susan. "Doggie here is one of the best pilots I know, and a bloody good singer. Get him to give you some acapella tunes on the flight."

She smiled and held out her hand. "Just so long as he doesn't get lost on the way back."

The male agent said nothing. He remained sullen to the end, quickly climbing into the cockpit, followed by Susan.

Gus waved them off and then headed over to the Davidstow officers' mess. It was time for breakfast. He spotted Billy sitting alone at a table, picked a newspaper off the stand where the dailies were stored and walked over to him. "Mind if I join you?"

"Not at all. They get off all right, Bouncer?"

"Yes, all in order," said Gus, opening the morning newspaper and scanning the front page. "Bloody hell," he said, staring at the headline. "Listen to this, Billy. There's been another blackout murder in London, an RAF officer this time."

"My God," said Billy. "I thought the Blackout Killer had been caught and executed?"

"That's right, he was. Leading Aircraftman Gordon Cummins — I remember it clearly. He was hanged at Wandsworth Prison back in June."

"So there's another murderer? Does the paper name the poor sod who was killed?" asked Billy.

Gus quickly scanned the rest of the article. "No. It just says the victim was a male officer, and that the body was found near Regent's Park."

"Unlikely to be anyone we know then," said Billy.

Gus didn't answer. He was deep in thought. The park wasn't that far from the Baker Street SOE office.

"The name will come out in due course," he said. "Anyway, what's for breakfast? I'm ravenous."

After breakfast, Gus and Billy went their separate ways, but at ten-thirty a call came to the mess, summoning Gus over to the Intelligence Office. When he got there, Billy Balsdon was waiting for him.

"Had an urgent call from a Wing Commander Peacock. Said you would recognise the name. He's instructed you to go to London immediately."

"What? That's nonsense. Let me call him back."

"As you like, but he seemed pretty agitated to me."

Gus found the number of Peacock's office and dialled it. The wing commander answered, and Gus tried to explain his difficulty. "Sir, I'm ordered to wait here until my Lizzie is fixed, then take it back to Tempsford."

"And I am countermanding that order," said an angry Peacock. "Forget the damned kite; someone else will fly it home. I'm ordering you to report to me at Baker Street tomorrow morning, as early as possible."

Gus put the phone down. He looked at Billy. "Looks like we'll have to have that game of squash another time," he said. "I've got to get back to London for an early meeting tomorrow morning."

"Oh, that's a pity, Bouncer. I was looking forward to it. But wait a minute — I've got an idea. You can stay here today and get the night train," said Billy. "I'll drive you over to Liskeard, and you can catch it there. It will get you into Paddington with enough time to get breakfast, and then you can get off to your meeting."

Gus considered this. "Sounds like a plan. What time have you booked the court for?"

"Seventeen hundred hours. And I've got some kit you can borrow. There." He pointed to a sports bag in the corner of his office. "Take it now, if you like."

The borrowed gym shoes pinched his toes, but that was no excuse. Gus just couldn't keep pace with Billy on the Davidstow court.

In rally after rally, Billy dominated the tee in the centre of the court. In fact, it seemed to Gus that Billy simply stood there, placing the ball into alternate corners of the court whilst he, Gus, sprinted from corner to corner, wearing himself out in no time.

After the first game, Billy looked at Gus, who was red-faced, gasping for breath and sweating profusely. He smiled. "Tell you what, Bouncer old chum," he said, "I'll play left-handed, shall I? Might even things out a tad."

Gus was nonplussed.

"I'm serious," said Billy.

They carried on, Billy playing left-handed. It was, nevertheless, a whitewash. Billy won all six games they played, with Gus only managing to take the odd point off him.

"Thanks for the game, Squashed Balls. I can see you've played a lot."

"A bit, yes. Learned the game at Harrow, then played at Corpus Christi. I was university champion three years running. Unofficially, of course."

Gus showered, dressed and recovered. Later, as promised, Billy drove him to Liskeard, where he caught the last train of the day bound for Paddington. Though he managed to get a whole compartment to himself, Gus got little sleep on the train, which clattered and stuttered all the way to London.

The next morning, Gus was stiff and sore. This was partly due to the cramped seat on the train; there had been no sleeper berths. But he was sure it was mostly the aftereffects of playing squash. He walked out of the station and onto Praed Street, stopping for breakfast at a small, streetside cafe. He ordered bacon and toast with coffee. When it arrived, the bacon was cold, and the coffee appalling. He should have gone for builders' tea, which most of the other customers were drinking.

Gus arrived at 64 Baker Street at 0930 and rang the doorbell. An airman opened it. "Flight Lieutenant Beaumont for Wing Commander Peacock," he said, flashing his ID.

"Yes, sir. Know the way up, sir?"

"Yes, I do," he said. Gus bounded up the stairs and knocked loudly on Peacock's door.

"Come on in," called Peacock. "Ah, Gustaw," he said, using Gus's given name. "So nice of you to be early. Do sit down."

"What's all this about?" asked Gus.

"It's Titus Grindlethorpe," said Peacock. "He's been murdered."

"What? Oh my God. The blackout killing in yesterday's papers — it was Grindlethorpe?"

"It seems so, yes. He didn't turn up for work on Friday, which is unusual. Later, the police came round to the office. They wanted someone to identify a body; I was off sick, but they called me in."

"The RAF Police?" asked Gus.

"No. Scotland Yard are investigating the case."

"Is that usual?"

"Apparently it is, yes. A murder committed anywhere in London, apart from on RAF property, is their territory."

"Even if the victim is military?"

"Yes."

"And the civilian police are sure it's him?"

"I went to the mortuary with a detective inspector. Sam Ruskin, he's called. He's leading the investigation. I identified the body. It was Titus, all right. His head had been bashed about quite a bit, but I could see it was him. We didn't want it in the papers, to be honest, considering the work Titus had been doing in the SOE. I'd prefer the RAF Police to investigate the whole thing. But for now, Detective Inspector Ruskin will be overseeing the case. We'll just have to wait and see what he comes up with. Now, to business. I have some more bad news for you, Gustaw. You're being taken off Special Ops."

"What?"

"Just for a short while. That business just now, getting lost over France and landing in Cornwall. Almost pranged the kite, I'm told…"

"Who told you that? Was it that Joe? The man? It's a bloody exaggeration."

"That's as may be, but still, you need a bit of rest, Gustaw. No disgrace in it. It's been a long, hard war. You've been in the thick of it right the way through."

"Are you grounding me?"

"No. Not exactly."

"What then?"

"I want you to go up north for a while. RAF Elvington — it's near York. There's a Free French heavy bomber squadron moving there as we speak, and it needs a liaison officer attached. Just the job for you, Gustaw."

"Free French Bombers?"

"Oh, don't look at me like that. I'm sure your French is up to it."

Gus looked crestfallen. Yes, he'd not been up to his best with the navigation, but it wasn't his fault the Lizzie had been attacked by a German night fighter. And what was this about him almost pranging the Lysander? Ridiculous.

"Needn't be for long," said Peacock, "and you're not grounded. Just no solo flights for the time being."

"Oh, I see. You mean I can be taken for a joyride in a Lancaster."

"Lancaster? You should be so lucky. No, the French squadron is equipped with the Short Stirling. Oh, and Gustaw, I want you to go up there today, on the next available train. I'll phone through and have someone pick you up at York station. And I'll arrange to have your kit sent over from Tempsford as soon as possible."

"If I'm going to do this liaison job properly," said Gus, "I need information about the squadron."

"Of course." Peacock opened his desk drawer and took out a file. He handed the paper to Gus. "Read this on the train up to York."

CHAPTER 7

Gus caught a train to York the same afternoon. He found a seat in the corner of a quiet carriage and, as the train steamed out of King's Cross, took out the file Peacock had given him.

Status — secret
September 1942
Thiès Squadron, Free French Air Force.

Background: The first French airmen left Bordeaux-Mérignac Airport and flew to England in June 1940, five days before the French Government capitulated and signed an armistice treaty with Germany.

Soon after, others, in both France and French North Africa, began to rally to de Gaulle's call. The growth in numbers of French airmen who have made the decision to fight against the Vichy regime has continued since then.

In addition, Free French officials have been recruiting in South America (Uruguay, Argentina and Chile) and a smaller cohort of volunteers has been established there. French forces in Cameroon and Chad in French Equatorial Africa have also rallied to the Gaullist cause.

Command: In the summer of 1940, de Gaulle named Colonel Martial Henri Valin as commander-in-chief. Valin took almost a year to move from the French military mission in Rio de Janeiro to the UK. He took up office in July 1941.

Strength: From an initial strength of around five hundred, the Free French Air Force had doubled by 1941. Around three hundred of these were stationed in England. Initially, whilst air crews were French, ground crew were almost exclusively British. In July 1941, the arrival in the Middle East of the former Aéronavale ground crew from Tahiti was a substantial boost to the French-speaking maintenance crews.

The Groupe de Bombardement (of which Thiès Squadron is part) was formed in 1941, initially equipped with Bristol Blenheim medium bombers. The Groupe and Squadron provided support to ground offensives against the Italians in North Africa. Thiès Squadron is due to convert to Short Stirling heavy bombers in August 1942 in preparation for re-siting to England in October.

Having read the report on the Free French Squadron, Gus settled down for the remainder of the journey north. He tried to nod off but found that he couldn't.

When he arrived, he saw a grey RAF car standing outside the station. A young woman in a Women's Auxiliary Air Force uniform stood by it. Gus walked over.

"Flight Lieutenant Beaumont, sir?" asked the WAAF.

"That's me," he answered, taking in her friendly smile.

"I'm your driver."

"How long will it take to reach Elvington?"

"Oh, about half an hour, sir. Do jump in."

Gus opened a door and slung the bag containing what little kit he was carrying onto the back seat. Then he sat in the front, beside the WAAF. She could only be nineteen or twenty, but he noticed that she was a more than competent driver.

"How long have you been based at Elvington?" he asked her.

"Ever since I completed basic training. That was two years ago."

"I suppose you've seen some changes."

"Not so many. The station was originally a grass airfield. Last year it was entirely reconstructed with three hardened runways. It's only just re-opened. Personnel comes and goes, of course."

Reconstructed with hardened runways replacing the grass — that was to take the heavy bombers, thought Gus. The grass strips were fine for light aircraft such as Lizzies and most fighters, at least when they weren't waterlogged. But they just wouldn't stand up to the pounding they got from medium and heavy bombers.

"And are there many French there yet?"

"Only the headquarters at the moment. But we're expecting the rest to arrive soon. Two squadrons of Stirlings, I've been told."

"That sounds about right," said Gus.

"Deathtraps, the riggers call them."

"What?"

"Those Stirlings. They're deathtraps."

"Why do you say that?"

"My friend Gerry says so. He's a rigger. Gerry says they have a hydraulic throttle control, which means they're slow to respond. It can be very dangerous during take-off, Gerry says."

"I'm sure the pilots can cope with that."

"Then there's the short wingspan. Short by name and short by nature, says Gerry."

"And what's the problem with that?"

"Gerry says they can't get up high enough to escape the German anti-aircraft fire because of their short wings. And something to do with the undercarriage. What are you going to be doing here, sir?" she asked, as she swung the car right off the Hull Road and towards Elvington.

"I'm to be the liaison officer to the French bomber squadrons. Where have you been ordered to take me, by the way?"

"To the mess. I mean, the British officers' mess, of course. The French have set up their own in one of the Nissen huts. There should be somebody there to meet you."

The land surrounding York and Elvington was flat. In fact, the whole journey from London had been marked by largely flat, featureless landscapes. That was why so many heavy bomber squadrons were based in East Anglia and East Yorkshire, Gus supposed.

Eventually they drove onto the base and showed their passes, and the WAAF drove up to a single-storey, redbrick building.

"Here we are, sir," she said, pulling up and jumping out to help Gus with his kit.

"Thanks," he said, reaching for his bag and turning towards the mess.

The car drove off. Gus went into the mess and was greeted by a flight lieutenant of about his own age.

"You must be Beaumont?"

"That's right. Gus, or Bouncer to my friends."

"Pleased to meet you," said the officer. "I'm Gordon James. Jimmy in the mess. I'm with 77 Squadron — adjutant to the station commander, Group Captain Whitworth. You're here to liaise with the French, I believe?"

"That's right."

"Well, good luck is all I can say."

"Oh?"

"Their HQ are the only ones here, including their catering staff, but what a stuck-up lot! Good luck, Bouncer."

"I suppose I'd better meet their commanding officer as soon as possible. Can you fix that for me, please, Jimmy?"

"Already onto it, old son. Tomorrow morning at 0900, in Commandant Pascale's office. WAAF Parry who drove you here will show you round. I've put her at your disposal for the first couple of weeks," said Jimmy. "I'll get an orderly to show you to your quarters. Dinner is at nineteen hundred hours sharp. You have a couple of hours to relax beforehand. Whitty, that's the CO, is away at the moment, but he says he'll invite you round to his place for drinks one night when he's back. All right?"

"Yes, perfectly. See you soon, Jimmy."

The adjutant turned to go.

"Oh, Jimmy, just one thing."

"Yes?"

"Do you fly Short Stirlings?"

"Not bloody likely. Deathtraps, they are. My squadron's on Halifaxes, much better kites."

"Have you flown Stirlings?"

"No. Talk to David Barnes if you want to know about flying the Stirling. You'll find him in the mess. Got to rush, bye."

"Bye, Jimmy."

As Jimmy departed, an orderly arrived to take Gus to his room. It was small, but Gus thought it charmingly cosy. For a room in a mess, anyway. It had a bed and a wardrobe, a window looking out towards the Nissen huts, which comprised most of the accommodation on the base, and a small desk in front of the window. There was an open fire, too. Somebody, probably the orderly, had set and lit the fire so that warmth issued from the glowing coals.

"Thanks for getting the fire going," Gus said.

"No problem, sir. It gets proper cold hereabouts, and we all like a bit of comfort when we can get it," said the orderly.

"Is there an officer called Barnes based here?"

"Flying Officer Barnes? Yes, sir. Nice man is young Mr Barnes. His quarters are just over on the other side of the dining room, sir. Would you like me to take him a message from you?"

"No. No thanks, that won't be necessary. I'll find him myself, later. That's all for now, Aircraftman… Oh, I'm so sorry, I didn't catch your name."

"Aircraftman Hopkins, sir. Bert, sir."

"Well, that's all for now, Bert. Thank you."

"No problem, sir."

"And no need for formalities in the mess, eh?"

"No. Thank you, Mr Beaumont."

Gus slumped onto the bed. He badly needed forty winks before dinner in the mess. He lay there, thinking about the murder of his former CO. He wondered when Grindlethorpe had been killed. What had Peacock said about the timing? Grindlethorpe hadn't turned up at the office on Monday. Or was it Friday? Gus had spoken to Grindlethorpe on Thursday evening. *Oh my God*, he thought. If he'd been killed on the Thursday night, Gus might have been one of the last people to see him alive.

He turned over onto his side. *Oh*, he thought, *and I have to write to Eunice*. Perhaps he was being daft. Of course Eunice would want to settle down once they were married, wouldn't she?

An hour later, Gus was still awake. He just couldn't drift off. It was becoming a much more frequent occurrence. What was the matter with him?

CHAPTER 8

Gus walked into the mess dining room and glanced around. There were six other officers there, standing around the bar. Jimmy wasn't one of them. One wore the same flight lieutenant braids as Gus; four others were pilot officers. There was just one flying officer present. Was it David Barnes, he wondered?

"Attention, everyone! New boy in the mess!" shouted the flight lieutenant. "Get him a bloody drink, and quick!"

"I'm Paddy," said one of the pilot officers, offering his hand to Gus. "What will you have?"

Gus shook Paddy's hand. "I'll have beer, please. Bitter."

"Nonsense," said the flight lieutenant. "Gin and tonics between eighteen-thirty and dinner. Won't allow anything else. And this one's on me. A gin and tonic for the officer, Barney — make it a double. And another one for myself. Oh, sod the cost, G and Ts all round!" Turning to Gus, he said, "Sandy Borringdon, at your service. And you are?"

"Gus Beaumont. Bouncer. Pleased to meet you. Pleased to meet all of you."

The flying officer was David Barnes, and after a pleasant dinner Gus quizzed him about the virtues of the Stirling bomber.

"I like the kite," said David. "I flew them with 214 Squadron. Once airborne, the Stirling is a delight to fly. Surprisingly manoeuvrable for such a large aircraft. I'd say it's more manoeuvrable and responsive than any other aircraft in its class, certainly more manoeuvrable than a Halifax. I've never flown a Lanc, mind."

"What about its ceiling? I been told it's quite low."

"That's true enough. It can't get much above sixteen-and-a-half thousand feet. It's the wings. They're too short, really. The original spec said the wings should be no more than a hundred feet wide, to fit into existing hangars. Bloody short-sighted, if you ask me."

"It can't get above the flak ceiling then?"

"No. Best to just speed through any flak with fingers crossed. On the other hand, it can out-turn a Ju-88 night fighter. A Halifax can't do that. Remember, the Stirling was chosen for the formation of the RAF's Pathfinder squadrons."

"Was it? I didn't know that. Interesting. I was also told the take-off can be a bit of a challenge."

"It can be a bit of a handful on take-off. And landing. More so for inexperienced pilots. It's the hydraulic throttle control. There can be a bit of a lag, which means they're slow to respond. But all four-engined heavies are demanding on the runway. They all swing due to prop torque, so the pilot needs to have the port and starboard engines running at different speeds to compensate. Why they don't make contra-rotating props, I don't know."

"Cost, I expect."

"Maybe. Anyway, if all four throttles are advanced simultaneously, the Stirling swings to the port and can become uncontrollable. That can collapse the landing gear, which can be bloody disastrous if the aircraft is loaded with bombs and fuel. The trick is to feed in the correct amount of throttle during the first twenty seconds of the take-off run. More left engines than right to balance the swing. Once the rudder becomes effective, all's well."

"Sounds like a handful."

"As I say, once she's up, she's a beauty."

"Anything else I need to know about the Stirling?"

"Why are you so interested?" asked David.

"I've been told that the two French squadrons I'm working with are equipped with them. That's all."

"Oh, I see. Well, in that case, all the pilots will have done the special training and certification programme for the Stirling. Flight engineers will have been fully briefed, too."

"In addition to familiarisation?"

"Yep. A series of serious accidents on take-off resulted in lots of total right-offs and a number of seriously injured crew. The RAF, in its infinite wisdom, put on this special course."

"Why's it so difficult? I want to know the detail, David. I need to be on a par with these chaps. Or a step ahead."

"There's the prop swing, as I said. But that's the case with the Halifax and Lancs, too, to an extent. It's also another effect of the Stirling's particularly short wingspan. In the prototype, the wingspan was too short to generate enough lift for take-off. The designers at Shorts decided to make the wing much thicker than usual."

"To get more elevation?"

"Yes. The thicker wing made it fly better but still didn't generate enough lift for a decent take-off. More tweaks were needed. The wing's angle of attack…"

"You mean angle of incidence. I do know the term — I'm a pilot, remember."

"Sorry. Yes, the angle of incidence had to be increased to generate more lift for take-off. But if the wing itself were to be modified, the Stirling would end up cruising with a nose-down attitude. Not good. Bit like the Whitley — you know the one?"

"Yes."

"So, the designers decided to increase the length of the front undercarriage. This tilted the nose up on take-off. Simple."

"And it worked?"

"It worked, yes, but it gave the Stirling its long, spindly landing gear. And an appallingly bad view forward from the cockpit."

"So, they solved one problem but created another?"

"You could say that. All of the factors I've mentioned club together to make take-off and landing particularly difficult, and contributed to many of the accidents."

"Hence the special course."

"There you have it, Bouncer. Like I said, the Stirling is difficult to take off and land, but once airborne, it's not a bad bird at all."

A half-length mirror was mounted on the back of the door of Gus's tiny room in the officers' mess. As he stood before it, he wiped away specks of dust from the corner of the glass.

It was the second day of his posting to RAF Elvington and he was about to go and meet the officer commanding the French Squadron, Commandant Pascal Pascale.

He wore a freshly ironed shirt and, looking in the mirror, ensured his necktie had the best Windsor knot that he could manage. Having brushed it meticulously, he put on his tunic and buttoned it up. He wanted to look his best.

Gus took a deep breath, grabbed his side-hat and walked out of the door. The young WAAF driver was there, waiting. Had Jimmy said she was called Parry?

"Do we need to drive?" he asked.

"The commandant's office is over on the other side of the base, sir, and we can't walk over the strip as the first of the French bombers are due soon. Better we drive around the perimeter, sir."

"All right, you've persuaded me. And look, please can we cut the formalities, at least when no one else is around? It's so tiresome."

"Yes, Mr Beaumont."

"And you are?"

"Isobel Parry. Izzy."

"Right then, Izzy. Let's get going, shall we?"

Izzy drove quickly around the outer edge of RAF Elvington. Gus gazed on the bombers of 77 Squadron. Most were Handley Page Halifax four-engined heavy bombers, but some of the smaller Armstrong Whitworth Whitleys the squadron had been previously equipped with had survived. They made a mighty show, and Gus could only imagine what it might be like to fly in one of dozens of similar aircraft, all in loose formation, and all aiming to drop their load of bombs on one enemy target.

Soon Izzy had stopped the car outside a low building. The unfamiliar Cross of Lorraine flag was flying from the top of a flagpole. Gus had done his homework, and he knew the Free French had adopted this as their own. The building was guarded by an airman wearing RAF uniform with Free French shoulder tabs and topped by a kepi.

Gus got out of the car.

"Good luck," said Izzy, smiling and saluting him.

Gus returned her smart salute. He turned to the guard, who also saluted. "*S'il vous plaît, le Capitaine Beaumont chez le Commandant Pascale,*" said Gus, summoning the best French accent he could muster.

"*Tout de suite, monsieur,*" said the guard. He called inside, and another airman came out to take Gus through to Pascale's office.

The office was of medium size and dominated by a large, polished walnut desk. On the desk were two miniature flags, one the French tricolour and the other the Free French cross.

On the wall behind the desk was a large photograph of General Charles de Gaulle. Pictures of Paris, featuring the Avenue des Champs-Élysées and the Eiffel Tower, decorated the other walls.

Pascale was seated. His face was that of a proud veteran: wrinkled and moustached. His piercing, light blue eyes gleamed behind his spectacles. He wore a dark blue uniform badged with French insignia. His braids of rank pointed upwards, unlike those of the RAF. Over his left breast pocket were a string of ribbons. Gus recognised two: the 1914–18 Inter-Allied Victory Medal and the green and red of the 1914–18 Croix de Guerre. Above these were pilots' wings.

Gus stood to attention and saluted. Pascale rose from his chair and returned the salute.

"*S'il vous plaît, asseyez-vous,*" he said, pointing to a chair under the picture of the Champs-Élysées. "*Je parle un peu anglais, mais votre français est probablement meilleur.*"

"*Bien sûr.* My French is a little rusty, but I hope you find it adequate."

"I am sure I shall, Monsieur Beaumont. A French name, I notice."

"Yes. Originally de Beaumont, I believe. It's an English surname, these days, but of Norman origin. My father's family were descended from Robert de Beaumont, the First Earl of Leicester. But that was a long, long time ago, naturally."

"Naturally. And your mother's family?"

"My mother was Polish. She and my father met when he was serving in the British Embassy in Warsaw."

"You have pedigree, Beaumont. That is good."

"Thank you, sir."

"Now, to business. Tell me, how do you view your role with my squadron?"

That's got straight to the crux, thought Gus. "It is very simple," he said. "I am here to ease your officers' stay in England, until the war is won. To be the interface between yourself and the station commander, Group Captain Whitworth. And, if it pleases you and your officers, to introduce them to the local delights in their free time. York is a wonderful city. Full of history and —"

"What do you know of history?" Pascale cut in.

"I studied history at Oxford before the war, sir."

"Then we have something in common. I taught history at the Collège de France."

"Then you must know the founders of the *Annales* school. Marc Bloch and Lucien Febvre?"

"Of course. You've read their works?"

"Yes. And I met Monsieur Bloch. Twice, in fact."

"You've met the master? Do tell me more."

"The first time was before the war. He gave a guest lecture in England. I was lucky enough to be there. It was fascinating. I met him again during the war…"

"You met him in wartime?"

"Yes. We crossed the Channel together in the same steamer. In 1940, from Dunkirk."

"What a small world. Look, I don't have much time. My flyers are due soon. I have to tell you, many of my pilots are affronted at being allocated the worst heavy bombers in the country."

"The Stirling can out-turn the German night fighters and has been selected by the RAF for Pathfinder work," he said, remembering what David had told him. "I assume your pilots have completed the special training and certification programme for Stirlings?"

"Yes, they have. Oh well, we'll just have to get on with it, won't we? But look here, Flight Lieutenant, I will have no interference in Thiès Squadron's affairs from you British. No interference. Thiès takes orders from your HQ, but how we enact those orders is up to us and us alone. Is that understood?"

"Yes, sir. Perfectly," said Gus.

"Good. In that case, I would like to invite you to dine with Thiès Squadron's officers tomorrow evening, meet some of the crews. Our mess is inside one of those miserable huts — what do you call them?"

"Nissen huts."

"But we've made the most of it. Will you join us? I know my officers will have brought some decent wine with them."

"Of course. I'd love to, but I'm sorry, I don't have my mess dress with me."

"No need for that. It won't be a black tie. Just wear the best version of uniform you have. We eat at twenty hundred hours; arrive half an hour before."

Gus stood to salute Pascale. The older man returned his salute and, as he did, they both heard the steady drone of engines as the first of the squadron's Stirling bombers arrived and prepared to land on the Elvington runway.

CHAPTER 9

The roar of three powerful engines filled the sky above RAF Elvington, announcing to everyone on the base that the mighty Stirling bombers of Thiès Squadron were making their arrival. Gus and David were standing by the control tower to watch the landings. The noise flooded over the base as the bombers circled the airfield once. In close linear formation, the Stirlings turned into wind and, following the lead aircraft, landed in succession.

The last of the three Stirlings approached, hanging low in the sky above the landing strip. Gus frowned, sensing something was wrong.

The pilot was a few seconds late in executing his flare for landing. The heavy aeroplane hit the runway hard and careered to port alarmingly. As the ground crews watched, the pilot regained control before the bomber fell off the strip.

"That was close."

"That's nothing," said David, "you'll get used to it."

The remainder of the squadron flew in the following day. This was also when the squadron's ground teams arrived. Trucks and buses full of men and kit poured in through Elvington's main gates. Gus glanced at the officers, guessing which ones he would meet in their mess later.

In reality, there was little at Elvington for Gus to do. He was becoming bored. In the afternoon, Izzy Parry drove him into York, where he found a very well stocked army and navy store.

"How can I help you, sir?" asked the shop assistant.

"I'm after a handheld compass."

"Of course, sir. The best I have is Prismatic Mark III. British-made, of course. It's made of solid brass, painted over in black, and has a mother-of-pearl dial which glows in the dark. It's very accurate, sir."

"I'll take one, please. And I need a decent torch."

"I'd recommend an American model, sir. The TL-122 flashlight, as the Yanks call them, is used by the US Army. It shows a very good light, is suitably robust and can easily be clipped to the clothing."

"Sounds good."

"Anything else, sir?"

"No, thanks. That's everything."

Once he'd shopped for what he needed, Gus returned to where Izzy was waiting with the car.

"Time to get back to Elvington, Mr Beaumont?" she asked as he walked towards her.

"Fancy a bite to eat, Izzy?" he asked. "I'll treat us."

"Oh, yes please."

"Where's best?"

"Betty's Café is by far the best. Does food all day long. It was hit by an incendiary bomb earlier this year, but an off-duty van driver who was acting as a fire watcher that night spotted it and raised the alarm."

"You lead the way, then," he said.

As they walked through the streets towards Betty's, Gus noticed people glancing at them. He wondered whether it was in order for him to be taking her out. After all, there was a massive difference in their ranks, and he assumed he was a few years older than Izzy. Moreover, he was engaged to Eunice. But they were only going out for tea and cake. He'd accompanied Susan for drinks in that Cornish pub. It was all quite innocent.

At Betty's they drank tea, ate cake and chatted. *What normal things to do*, Gus thought. *And in the middle of a war.* But York was unlike London. Perhaps it was the Yorkshire city's distance from the continent. Though still within the range of German bombers, the distance meant they were at the end of their capacity, weren't escorted by fighters and, anyway, the RAF was now in a much better position to defend against their attacks than it had been in 1940 and '41.

The so-called Baedeker Blitz had taken place earlier that year, in April. The Nazis' decision to hit York was probably in retaliation for the RAF's raid on Lübeck in March. Some people thought York had been chosen for its historical and cultural heritage, but on the night the targets had been strategic: the railway station, the carriage works, the airfield. There had been no further raids for months, since August in fact, when a lone raider had dropped four bombs on the city centre.

Once back at Elvington, Gus had a stroll around the three Stirlings parked up beyond the control tower. They were gigantic, the largest aeroplanes Gus had seen, and the cockpit sat at a great height from ground level. In between viewing the comings and goings of aircraft and crews, and some feeble attempts at doing some admin, Gus wrote to Eunice.

When he was finished, Gus lay back on the bed and read the letter through:

Dear Eunice,

I trust all is well — and you are not too cold, my darling — up there in Bonnie Scotland. How are Mr and Mrs Farquhar? Well, I hope. Do give them my very best wishes. Have they heard from Duncan at all?

How are the wedding preparations going? I can't wait for news.

Did you read the news about Grindlethorpe? Crikey, what next?

A bit of bad news here, I'm afraid. I've been grounded by Peacock. Well, not exactly 'grounded' and certainly not for any misdemeanour. I made a bit of a mess of navigating home the other day, and Peacock thinks I need a rest. A bit of R and R, so to speak. He's moved me to RAF Elvington, up near York. I went into the city this morning, actually. It's very nice — I'm sure you'd love it. I bought a nice brass compass. It's good quality. I'm not going to be caught out again!

On the plus side, RAF Elvington is much closer to you, darling. Perhaps I could come up once I get a spot of leave. It's much closer than Tempsford. Or you could take the train down to York and I'll get one of the cars and pick you up. Today, after picking up the compass, I went for tea and a nice cake in a delightful tearoom called Betty's. I'll take you when you visit.

I'm sure you'll like it here. There are lots of gallant Free French Air Force officers, and I'm their liaison officer.

I've had time to think about us and our future together once we are married. I'd always imagined that we'd start a family straight away; I know you simply adore children. I'd also thought that you'd prefer to live in Winchester rather than London. It would certainly be safer for you, and any babies we have.

But I realised just the other day that we haven't really spoken about it, so I don't know what your thoughts on the subject are. Of course, the war affects everything — without it, things would be much more straightforward. But we are where we are, and we're not the only ones. Thinking of Milly Turner in Manchester with Tunio's child, and on her own now, I wonder if perhaps we ought to wait? And what about you? Are you thinking of returning to work as a Joe again, or have you had it with all that? We really do need to talk these things through. I hope you agree.

Well, I have to stop now, dearest. I'm invited to the French officers' mess tonight, a sort of 'dining in', I think. They want to get the measure of me and my French, so wish me luck.

Miss you lots and love you to the moon and back, Eunice. Hope to see you again very soon.

Your dearest, ever loving Gus XXX

SWALK

He folded the letter so that it was a quarter of its original size. He placed it inside an envelope, which he sealed down and addressed to Eunice, care of Duncan's parents' address. Then he stuck a stamp onto the top right-hand corner. He'd pop it into the post on his way to the mess.

CHAPTER 10

Each Stirling bomber of the French squadron had a crew of seven, a mix of commissioned officers and NCOs. As in the RAF, officers and other ranks had separate social, eating and sleeping arrangements.

The French officers' mess at RAF Elvington was inside one of the many Nissen huts that cluttered the station, and in the darkness of late evening Gus was marching across the hardstanding towards it.

Unlike English and Polish, which he'd learnt from his parents as a child, Gus had studied French and German at school in Winchester. By the time he'd left school and progressed to Oxford, both were 'adequate' at best. He still spoke French like an English public-school boy, and he hoped to God Pascale didn't invite him to make a speech.

Gus poked his head through the door and gazed at the scene before him. The inside of the mess was constricted by the curved shape of the Nissen hut's ceiling, which followed the roof's profile. Along both sides of the mess were lounge furnishings: an Art Deco style sofa and chair, a wooden writing bureau and a walnut-veneered piano. There were rugs on the floor and he noticed a ginger tomcat under the bureau. On the wall at the end of the room was a tiled fireplace with a clock on the mantelpiece. Above this were two flags. The one on the right was a blue, white and red tricolour, a red Cross of Lorriane emblazoned on the white stripe. On the left was a flag Gus didn't recognise, perhaps the squadron's colours. Beneath the flags was a map of France. To the left of these flags was a large picture of the Arc de Triomphe and on the right, a similar sized picture of Montmartre at night.

The table was covered in a white, starched cloth and set for dinner. A wheeled trolley containing a decanter of golden-coloured spirit, probably cognac, stood ready at the side.

Gus introduced himself to the airman on the door, who made a grand and very loud announcement of his arrival to all and sundry. Pascale heard and turned towards him. "Ah, Monsieur Beaumont," he greeted. "Come, come meet my officers."

Gus walked smartly over to where Pascale was drinking an aperitif with two younger men.

"Allow me to introduce Capitaine Soutine. Capitaine, this is Flight Lieutenant Gustaw Beaumont."

A young, dark-haired, rather squat officer offered his hand. "Pierre, please. Pleased to meet you, Gustaw."

"Gus," said Gus with a smile.

"And this is Capitaine Pinault," Pascale went on. "I'll leave you in their capable hands, if you don't mind." With that, he wandered over to talk to another small group of officers.

"Louis. Pleased to meet you, Gus," said Pinault, who seemed a lot older than Pierre. "Let me get you a drink. We are drinking pastis, but perhaps you don't like the taste?"

"A pastis would be lovely, thank you."

"What's your role here?" asked Pierre as Louis ordered three more glasses of pastis from the bar.

"I'm your liaison officer. Not much to do on base, obviously, as all your ground crew are French…"

"Not all of them, actually. Most. And many of the others speak French, at least."

"Anyway, I'm here to help sort out any issues you might have — you know the sort of thing."

"Will you fly with us?" asked Louis, drinks in hand.

"You wear pilot's wings," said Pierre. "You are a flyer?"

"Of course, but I'm not qualified to fly anything like a Stirling. Biggest thing I've flown is a Bristol Blenheim, bombing the Italians in Albania last year."

"Blenheims, eh? Rubbish planes," blurted Pierre.

"Flown them, have you?"

"Yes. After the capitulation, I moved to the Middle East to serve in a Free French flight. I was based at Haifa in Palestine. We were attacked by four Italian bombers. Only two of our planes got up, a fighter pilot in a Morane-Saulnier M.S.406…"

"That's a single-seat fighter," put in Louis.

"…and me. I got up in a Potez 631," Pierre continued. "Do you know the type?"

Gus shook his head. "No."

"Similar to a Blenheim, actually. A little smaller, designed for multirole: fighter, bomber or reconnaissance. The 631 I flew was fitted out as a day fighter. Rubbish plane, nearly as poor as a Blenheim. The Potez had a low maximum speed and a poor rate of climb compared with contemporary fighter aircraft, but it did have seven forward-firing machine guns, enough to see off those Italians. Soon after that I was redeployed to Fort Lamy in French Equatorial Africa. Then my unit merged with other flights into the 101st Groupe de Bombardement, and the Thiès Squadron as we are now. Our first British planes were Blenheims."

"Have you flown Blenheims, Louis?" asked Gus.

"No. I was a civilian pilot. I cut my teeth on a Dewoitine D.338, a passenger airliner. I flew on routes in Europe and on the service to Dakar via Casablanca. I was in West Africa when the war broke out. I got myself back to France to join up. I was put on bombers. The Farman F.220 was my bread and butter."

"Never heard of those," said Gus.

"Farmans are odd-looking kites. High-winged, four-engined monoplane with a retractable undercarriage. Unusually, the four engines are wing-mounted in two nacelles — one pulling and the other pushing the plane along."

"That is unusual!"

"Yes, it counters the prop torque pretty well, though. Anyway, get this: I had the privilege of leading one of the Republic's first raids over Germany in a Farman. Not bombs, though. Leaflet raids, they were! Then we were over Germany on night bombing raids in May and June 1940. I think there are still some Farmans knocking about. The bombers were relegated to transports and used by us and the Vichy regime."

"How did you get here?" asked Gus.

"I saw the writing on the wall and got over to England just after Dunkirk. Lots of us did. I speak very good English, actually, Gus."

"You do?"

"Yes. Here, let me ask you a question." Louis began to speak English. "Gus, why does a Frenchman only have one egg for his breakfast?"

"I don't know. Tell me."

"Because one egg is enough! Get it? One egg's an *oeuf*!" Louis broke into hysterical laughter.

"Does he tell a good joke?" asked Pierre.

"Not that good, actually. But as we say here in England, 'there's a war on' so it will do," said Gus with a smile.

"Look, dinner is arriving," said Louis. "Come sit with us. Let's see what the chef has come up with."

Considering the French had only just arrived, Gus thought the food was excellent — much better than he was used to. On the table as the officers sat was some sliced *saucisson* and *rillettes de porc* with bread, which they munched on whilst finishing the pastis. Next came a fish soup — *bourride* — with yet more bread and a couple of bottles of nice, crisp Muscadet.

The main course, accompanied by four bottles of Gamay, was a dish of white meat in a wine sauce. Pierre explained that the chef had a habit of trying to create a faux *blanquette de veau*, since he couldn't get veal. This one was chicken, but apparently pork had also been tried. After the main course came cheese and claret. Dessert was an apple tart accompanied by a sweet wine.

Unlike at Tempsford, there were no rough-and-tumble after-dinner games in the French mess. Instead, the entertainment was provided by a couple of airmen. A sergeant and corporal sat themselves in a corner by the fire as the cognac was poured. One had an accordion; the other was a singer.

They began with a medley of what Pierre called 'street music', followed by a rendition of the Charles Trenet song 'Boum!'

Pierre explained that Trenet had written this song for the film *La Route Enchantée*, which had been released the year before the war.

"It was very popular in France," whispered Pierre as the vocalist, a tenor, headed towards the refrain for a second time, "though Trenet has since disgraced himself in the eyes of the Free French by collaborating with the Germans."

Gus vaguely recognised the bright, jaunty tune. He listened to the lyrics, mentally translating them into English as he did so: *Boom! When my heart goes 'Boom!' Everything goes 'Boom!' with it, And it's love that awakens.*

The evening ended with a rousing performance of the French National Anthem led by the musicians. Everyone present, Gus included, stood to attention, right arm across chest, and the French officers sang lustily.

Leaning back in his seat, an unfiltered Gauloises cigarette in hand, Pierre turned to Gus and released a pungent cloud of smoke. "Tomorrow," he said, "you'll make your first flight in a Short Stirling. Come to aeroplane B — B for *Bravade* — for 0930. We'll meet you there."

As he tossed and turned in an effort to sleep, Gus couldn't stop wondering what tomorrow might bring. *B for Bravade*, he thought. *Bravado*. Pierre certainly had plenty of that.

CHAPTER 11

"Good morning, Gus," said Pierre, looking at his wristwatch. He was standing underneath the wing of one of Thiès Squadron's Stirlings. As Gus approached him, he saw the squadron code H7 in front of the roundel, followed by the aircraft identification letter 'B'.

"You are a little late. The rest of the crew are in position. We've been waiting for you."

"Sorry about that. I thought we agreed 0930."

"No. We agreed 0900 hours. Not to worry. Welcome to Stirling B for *Bravade*, Gus. Let's get aboard, shall we?"

Gus was embarrassed at his mistake, but he could have sworn 0930 was the agreed rendezvous time. He followed Pierre along the port side of the Stirling. Towards the aircraft's rear a small set of steps led up to an entrance. Pierre climbed in first, Gus following close behind.

Once up the steps, he stuck his head into the bomber and saw that this door opened directly onto the rear fuselage walkway.

"Come inside," urged Pierre, pointing to a second ladder. "That's the access up to the rear gun turret. Adjutant Le Blanc is our tail-end Charlie — all correct back there, François?"

"All correct, Capitaine!"

"This way, Gus," said Pierre, pointing to a door in the floor. "That's the ventral escape hatch. Let's hope we don't need it today. If we do, the operation is self-explanatory."

They continued forward along the walkway, their boots loud on the metal surface and echoing slightly. Inside, the Stirling smelt of bare metal, oil and grease. Clearly, the aeroplane's ventilation was poor. They soon came to another ladder, which went up to the mid-upper gun turret.

"You good up there, Robert?"

"All good, Capitaine," came the reply.

"That's Adjutant Assous," Pierre explained. "He's my most experienced crew member."

"What exactly is an adjutant? In your air force, I mean?" asked Gus.

"A senior NCO. Like a warrant officer in your military, I suppose. The accordion player last night, he's an adjutant, too. Come and meet the others."

They walked past yet another set of ladders, this one reaching up to the roof of the Stirling. Pierre pointed upwards. "Cabin roof escape hatch," he said, before going through a sliding door which led to a vast space situated in the middle of the Stirling, between the two wings.

They looked around. Pierre pointed again. "This is the crew rest bunk," he said. "Later, I'll send one of the boys back here so that you can have a front-row seat for take-off. By the way, I should have said that back near the ladder going up to François' rear gun turret is a chemical lavatory. It can get a bit uncomfortable up there when we're lurching around in turbulence or we're caught in an air-pocket. These large bombers don't behave in the same way as the aeroplanes you're used to. Not a luxury you're used to, I expect?"

"No, it isn't. I've got a reasonably sound stomach, though," said Gus.

"Good. You'll need it."

Gus had once flown as a navigator on an SOE mission to Poland and was quite used to large aircraft, but he was not going to say anything. Not if there was any chance of him getting airsick later, because, not for the first time, Gus felt as though the French were out to test him.

Yes, he thought, *it's a test.* The more he thought about it, the more he was convinced they had agreed to a 0930 start. They'd set him up — put him ill at ease from the word go.

As they moved further forward along the same level, Pierre stopped at a point where the front of the wings joined the Stirling's fuselage. Gus observed a wireless operator's station, where a very young-looking airman sat.

"Allow me to introduce our baby, Aspirant Xavier Monet," said Pierre, and the young officer blushed. "That's not fair of me. Xavier has recently finished cadet training but is not yet commissioned. To all intents and purposes, he is an officer. And a bloody good wireless operator, aren't you, Xavier?"

"I hope so, Capitaine."

"Allow me to introduce Gus Beaumont; he's the RAF officer attached to Thiès Squadron."

"Pleased to meet you, Gus."

"Likewise."

"You do appreciate the importance of the wireless operator, don't you, Gus?"

"You mean for navigation?"

"Yes. And bomb-aiming. Explain to him, Xavier."

"We use what's known as the GEE system. On large, fixed targets, such as cities, it gives enough accuracy to be used by itself as an aiming reference. Even at night, we don't need to use a bombsight or other external references. Of course, we still use other methods to double check, and because the Germans are beginning to use radio-jamming equipment. And yes, as you suggest, we use the wireless for general navigation purposes, especially when returning from a raid."

"Xavier also operates the nose gun turret when required. We're all a bit interchangeable, actually. Adjutant Blum here — " he pointed to an NCO who was sitting in front of a control panel on the starboard side of the compartment — "is the flight engineer but can also operate the wireless, can't you, Martin?"

"Yes, Capitaine, and the machine guns," the adjutant replied with a grin.

Behind Blum, on the port side of the compartment, Gus recognised a navigator's table.

"Lieutenant Laval here is navigator and bomb-aimer," said Pierre.

Gus nodded and smiled.

"Look there." He pointed to a set of steps going downwards. "Those are the access steps to both the nose machine guns and the bomb-aimer's position. If we suspect there are night fighters around, Xavier goes forward to the guns."

"How do you decide that?"

"They operate alongside the searchlights, but sometimes we wait until we see something in the air."

"Isn't it too late by then?"

"So, what do you think we should do?"

I've irritated him, thought Gus. He shrugged and remained silent.

"When we approach the target and can see it, illuminated, Martin goes down to do the bomb-aiming, a back-up to GEE. Now, come on up to the flight deck," Pierre continued, pointing out the storage spaces for parachutes and dinghies as they clambered past.

They climbed a couple of steps. Gus noticed how agile the French officer was around the aeroplane. He saw that the two pilots' seats and controls were contained within a fully glazed flight deck, which, because it was separate from everything else, had a relatively simple appearance. The control panel, on the other hand, looked complicated, with a vast array of display equipment for the pilots to take on board. *Lots of controls*, thought Gus, though probably no more than the twin-engined Lockheed Hudson the SOE were now using.

"Allow me to introduce my co-pilot, Sous-Lieutenant Marcel Poincare."

"Good morning," said Gus. "Thanks for having me aboard today."

The co-pilot gazed at him with antipathy. "*C'est la vie.*"

"Now," said Pierre quickly, moving on, "where can we sit you? I was going to send young Xavier back to the rest area so you could take his seat, but I've got a better idea. You shimmy down to the bomb-aimer's position, Gus. You'll have a fantastic view from there."

As he descended the steps that led down to the bomb-aimer's position in the lower nose of the Stirling, Gus heard Poincare laugh and mutter, "I hope you love the ride, Englishman."

This confirmed Gus's suspicion. He was on trial. The French were testing his resolve and his nerve.

He lay on his belly and gazed out through the Perspex. He listened to Pierre's orders through the RT as the Stirling's four engines were started up in sequence. The mighty roar of the fourteen-cylinder, Bristol Hercules radial engines was accompanied by a vibration that shook the bomber from nose to tail.

"Crew ready for take-off?" asked Pierre through the RT as the Stirling taxied out to the far end of the Elvington strip.

"Ready, Capitaine," they answered in turn.

"You ready, Gus?"

"Ready."

"Don't worry about the lack of belts down there," said Pierre. "It's only a short familiarisation flight."

At the end of the strip, Pierre turned the Stirling into what wind there was and applied the ground brakes. The roar of the engines immediately picked up and the heavy bomber began to trundle along the runway. Gus felt the Stirling being pushed to port.

"Increasing port engine revs," said Pierre.

"Roger," said Marcel.

The Stirling steadied as it increased speed. Gus felt the tail rise and knew that Pierre would now be able to use the rudder to keep the aeroplane straight.

"Full throttle on all engines," said Pierre.

"Roger."

Gus stared down at the runway as the bomber picked up speed. When would Pierre pull back on the stick and get her up in the air? *Blimey*, he thought, *this is the scariest thing ever.* Or was it? What about the time he'd been bounced by the Bf-109 over France in 1940? Or when he'd faced the might of the Luftwaffe onslaught during the Battle of Britian? He'd been frightened when he'd crash-landed that Blenheim on Corfu, convinced he would overshoot the small beach and career into the trees. Then there was the time he'd flown alone in the Fw-190 over the Dieppe beaches and back to England.

This was different. Gus was acutely aware he had no control over the situation. All he could do was lie there in the Stirling's bomb-aimer position and watch. He'd never been so frightened in his entire life.

Soon, the Stirling was airborne.

"Undercarriage up," ordered Pierre. "Want to come up on the flight deck, Gus?"

"Yes, please," he replied, gratefully.

"Marcel, you go back and keep the others company. Gus, get yourself up here."

He clambered up to the cockpit and got into the co-pilot's seat.

The Stirling gained height. Soon they were at ten thousand feet, and Pierre levelled off.

"Give me a course to take us over Hornsea," he said.

"One hundred degrees, Skipper," said the navigator.

"Would you like to take the controls?" asked Pierre.

"Why not?" answered Gus, placing both hands on the column.

Pierre let go. "She's all yours," he said. "I'll talk you through a few turns."

Under Pierre's guidance, Gus turned to port and flew the Stirling on an almost easterly course, which took them over Hornsea and out over the North Sea. Then he turned to port and flew northwards, parallel to the coast.

"Permission to test the guns?" called a voice.

"Carry on, François," said Pierre, and Gus heard the rattle of machine-gun fire from the tail. "You next, Robert. Xavier, go down and get ready to give the nose guns a blast."

Gus brought the Stirling round to starboard again until it was facing east and out to sea.

"I'll take the controls, Gus," said Pierre. "Let me show you what she's made of. Strap in, everyone."

Pierre put the Stirling through a series of twists and turns, corkscrewing the heavy aeroplane around the empty sky. He climbed then dived alarmingly, pulling out, banking left then corkscrewing again. Gus felt his stomach beginning to churn. *No, don't. Hold on*, he thought.

"Marcel, come back up here, would you? Gus, go back to the bomber's position, or sit back in the rest area, if you prefer."

Another bloody test, thought Gus. "Oh, I'll go forward," he said. "I just love the view from that position."

He didn't. He'd never felt so vulnerable. As Pierre and Marcel brought the Stirling into wind and set up their final approach to Elvington, Gus saw the runway coming up to meet him. He closed his eyes. There was a mighty banging sound accompanied by a heavy jolt as the bomber came down on its long, spindly main undercarriage, bounced once and settled. Soon the tail came down; Gus felt the Stirling lose speed and opened his eyes. *Crikey*, he thought. *I'm glad that's over.*

CHAPTER 12

Gus was in the mess enjoying a morning cup of tea when the phone rang. David Barnes answered it. "It's for you," he said to Gus, then whispered, "It's Jimmy James."

Gus strode over to the phone. "Morning, Jimmy. What's up?"

"I've got a Detective Inspector Ruskin from Scotland Yard here. He wants to speak to you. I don't know what this is about, but he looks mean. And he's got a snowdrop with him, so get over here quick!"

The phone went dead. Gus stared at the receiver, stunned.

David saw the look on his face. "Bad news, Bouncer?"

"No," lied Gus. "Got to dash, though — something about my former CO, I think." He rushed up the stairs to his room, picked up his side hat and sprinted back down, taking the steps two at a time. He ran through the mess doorway, calmed himself and marched over to the adjutant's office.

Izzy Parry was standing by one of the cars outside Jimmy's office. "Morning!" she called with a smile.

Gus simply nodded to her, took a breath, then knocked on Jimmy's door.

"Come in," Jimmy called, and Gus walked inside. He surveyed the room. Standing before him were Jimmy and an RAF flying officer sporting a uniform with a white stable belt, a white-topped peaked cap — hence the nickname snowdrop — and the red and black insignia of the RAF Police. Off to one side was an older, sharp-featured man in a pinstriped civilian suit and macintosh.

"Good morning, Flight Lieutenant Beaumont," said Jimmy, officiously. "I want to introduce you to Detective Inspector Ruskin. He's from London — Scotland Yard. The detective inspector has Group Captain Whitworth's permission to enter the station to talk to you, so long as he is accompanied by Flying Officer Anderson-Maggs, here."

The flying officer nodded towards Gus, who took in his stern face.

"You can use my office for as long as you need to, Detective Inspector," said Jimmy, looking at Ruskin. "I'll go now. If you need anything, ring this bell —" he pointed to a small handbell on the desk — "and one of my men will be here to take orders. Orders from Flying Officer Anderson-Maggs, that is. Everything clear?"

"Crystal clear, thank you," said Ruskin. His voice was rough and gravelly, and Gus thought he detected an East London accent.

Jimmy James left the room, and Gus wondered who was in charge. Was it the RAF policeman, Anderson-Maggs? Or Ruskin, the civilian?

"Shall we sit down?" asked Ruskin.

"I don't need to stay," said Anderson-Maggs. He looked at Gus. "Flight Lieutenant Beaumont, this has nothing to do with me or the RAF. I'm simply here to ensure proper protocols are upheld. I hope you understand."

"Yes, of course."

"Detective Inspector Ruskin, if you will excuse me, I have some administration to complete. If you need anything, just ring the bell. I'll be in the room next door."

"Certainly, thank you," said Ruskin. "Oh, just one thing before you go." He turned to Gus. "Would you like a cup of tea?"

Gus had just had one, but a hot drink might take some of the tension out of the situation. That was Ruskin's motive, of course.

"Yes please," he said.

"Flying Officer, please could you arrange for a pot of tea to be sent through?" said Ruskin. "Two cups, unless you want one yourself — in the room next door, of course."

"I don't," said Anderson-Maggs. He opened the door, walked out and called for a corporal. Gus heard him ordering the tea as the door sprang shut.

"I don't think the RAF want me here," said Ruskin, "do you?"

"Absolutely no idea."

"Let's take a seat. Smoke?" asked the detective inspector, taking a white packet of Senior Service from an inside pocket.

"I don't, thanks."

"Mind if I do?"

"Not at all."

Ruskin took a single cigarette from the packet. He took a match from a box which had appeared from nowhere, struck it and held the flame to the cigarette end. He breathed in, the smoke caught in the back of his throat, and he began coughing.

"Sorry," he said, recovering. "No. The Air Force doesn't want me here, but I'm investigating a civil crime. The murder of an RAF officer — Squadron Leader Titus Grindlethorpe. Did you know him?"

"I'm sure you must know that I did," said Gus.

"Better to just answer the questions, Flight Lieutenant Beaumont," Ruskin said, smiling. He took another pull on the cigarette and coughed again.

"Yes, I knew Grindlethorpe."

"When did you first meet him?"

"In 1939. He commanded my first squadron."

"And that was?"

"An army liaison outfit. We were sent to France soon after the outbreak of war."

"And you served in Squadron Leader Grindlethorpe's squadron until when?"

"Summer of 1940, just after Dunkirk. Then I left to join a fighter unit and stayed with fighters throughout the Battle of Britain."

Ruskin was jotting notes all the time that Gus spoke. He seemed to be an experienced detective, and Gus wondered how many murder investigations the policeman had worked on.

"And that was that, was it? You didn't come across him again?"

"That was it for a while. Later, after the Battle of Britian, I was posted to the Mediterranean theatre. First Greece, then Malta. I bumped into Squadron Leader Grindlethorpe again there. We were working at the same base, RAF Ta Kali. He wasn't my CO. He was in charge of defending the base. Searchlights, and ack-ack."

"How long were you based at Ta Kali?"

"About a month. Maybe a little longer. If you want precise dates, I'll have to go fetch my logbooks. It's been a busy war for some of us, you know."

"No need for that, Flight Lieutenant," said Ruskin. "I did my bit in the Great War. Navy. That's when I turned to these." He shook the packet of Senior Service cigarettes. "In any case, war or no war, Britian still needs policing. There are some bad 'uns around."

"Apologies. I shouldn't have said that. There was no need," said Gus.

There was a knock at the door, then Anderson-Maggs opened it and a WAAF came in with a tray containing a pot of tea, two cups, a milk jug, a sugar pot and a small plate of biscuits.

"Thank you," said Ruskin, resting his cigarette on an ashtray. "I'll be mother, shall I? Milk and sugar for you?"

"Just a drop of milk."

"I don't need to see your logbooks. Let's carry on. You worked with Squadron Leader Grindlethorpe a third time, back in London. That's correct, isn't it?"

"Yes."

"And you were both under Wing Commander Sir Alex Peacock's command?"

"Correct."

"When did you see Squadron Leader Grindlethorpe?"

"On Thursday the first of October."

"Where was that?"

"The SOE's library on Baker Street."

"And did you speak to him?"

"Not really — just to pass the time of day, comment about the weather. That sort of thing."

Ruskin stared at him silently.

"We weren't exactly on good terms."

"Did you like Squadron Leader Grindlethorpe, Flight Lieutenant?"

"No," answered Gus.

"May I ask why not?"

"He was officious, bumptious and bore grudges. Good at his work, in a pedantic sort of way, I suppose. But no, I didn't like him."

"Did you kill him?"

"No."

"Did Squadron Leader Grindlethorpe like you?"

"No, I don't think so."

"Why do you think he didn't like you?"

"When I was serving in Grindlethorpe's squadron, I pranged a Lysander. This was in 1940. I lost my gunner, a flight sergeant called Chester. He was a good man. I was shot down in another Lizzie a week or so later. I think Squadron Leader Grindlethorpe took a dislike to me then. As I say, he bore grudges."

"Is that all?"

"No. When we were flung together in Malta, Grindlethorpe kept up a vendetta against me."

"Is that when Stewart Poore was killed?"

"How on earth…?" Gus almost choked on his tea.

"Just answer the question. Was that when Flying Officer Poore died?"

"Yes."

"How did he die?"

"He was hit by our own ack-ack guns."

"Talk me through it. All of it, please."

"Stewart Poore and I had trained together very early on in the war. We became good friends. When I got to Malta, Stewart — 'Poorly' we called him — was there too. We were flying Hurricane night fighters out of RAF Ta Kali.

"That night, I was flying a patrol, wingman to Poorly. It was a bright night and the pair of us were patrolling the night skies over Valetta. Suddenly, his voice came over the RT. He'd spotted a bandit. I looked and saw a solitary Fiat Br-20 bomber. It was illuminated by our searchlights, and for once, the searchlight team were doing a good job of keeping the Italian aircraft in their beam. There it was, clear as clear could be.

"Poorly told me he was going after the bomber. It was my job to watch his back and keep an eye out for any other raiders. Poorly dived out of the night sky and his Hurricane closed in on the Fiat as I watched. He got closer and closer. Then, just as he had the Fiat in his sights and I judged he was close enough to open fire on it, bang! The air around the two aircraft exploded with flak, smoke and metal parts. It was carnage. The Italian and Poorly were blasted out of the sky. He didn't stand a chance."

Ruskin nodded. "So, just to be clear, both the Italian and Stewart Poore's Hurricane were shot down by British anti-aircraft fire from RAF Ta Kali?"

"Yes."

"Who was responsible for that fire?"

"How do I know? It's what happens in war. Sometimes."

"Who do you think was responsible?"

"When I landed, I jumped out of my kite and dashed over to the guns, demanding to see the officer commanding them. It was a young Royal Artillery lieutenant named McCann. I asked him which guns had opened fire. It was just his number four section, apparently. I asked McCann if he had given the order to fire. He told me he hadn't, because he could see the Hurricane was closing in and it was far too dangerous to open fire."

"Then who did order the fire?" insisted Ruskin.

"McCann and I talked to the NCO in charge of number four section. It was a sergeant called Harris. He insisted he had been given the order to open fire. The bomb-aimers and gunners backed him up. Many of them maintained they had also heard the order shouted out. McCann said Harris was a steady man and he was sure he was telling us the truth. I asked McCann who could possibly have given that order? Did he see anybody around? Anyone at all?"

"And what did Lieutenant McCann say?"

"He said that the only officer beside himself was Squadron Leader Grindlethorpe. He was doing his rounds as usual. I blamed Grindlethorpe and told him so."

"So, there were two distinct reasons for Squadron Leader Grindlethorpe taking a dislike to you?"

"Yes…" Gus hesitated.

"Something else?"

"Grindlethorpe was an anti-Semite. In the thirties, he was one of Oswald Mosley's supporters. I'm Jewish. At least, my mother was a Jew."

"And Grindlethorpe knew this, did he?"

"Yes, he did."

"I think we need a break," said Ruskin.

Gus left the office and headed outside into the fresh air. What he needed was time to think.

Did Detective Inspector Ruskin really believe he'd killed Grindlethorpe? Was Gus going to be charged? He tried to work out when the murder had taken place. News of this latest Blackout Murder had hit the papers on Monday. The Sunday before, Gus had been at Davidstow, with the Joes and Billy Balsdon to verify. Friday night into Saturday he could verify, too. He'd been on the Lysander pick-up. But how much of the sensitive information could he divulge, even to provide his own alibi?

He went back into Jimmy's office. Ruskin was there already, together with Anderson-Maggs.

"Shall we resume?" asked Ruskin, another cigarette in his fingers. He was already wheezing.

"Ready when you are."

Ruskin nodded to the RAF police officer, and the snowdrop left the room.

"What can you tell me about Operation Lodz?"

"Nothing."

"You don't know anything about it?"

"I was part of it."

"Then why can't you tell me about it?"

"Because I'm bound by the Official Secrets Act."

The detective looked up from his notes and considered this in silence. Gus could see that it had taken the wind out of his sails.

"And an officer called Krawiec?"

"Polish Air Force officer. Can't say more for the same reason. Sorry."

"And I don't suppose you can tell me much about Operation Jubilee, the Dieppe raid? Especially about a report drawn up by a French Resistance cell?"

"How do you know about that? And what has any of this got to do with Grindlethorpe's death?" Gus blurted out, instantly regretting his lack of control.

Ruskin took a drag on his cigarette. "When we searched Squadron Leader Grindlethorpe's flat, we found his diary. It makes interesting reading. Seems he thought somebody had been following him. Named a few names — possibilities, you might say. All very interesting. You see, Flight Lieutenant Beaumont, Grindlethorpe's killer is unlikely to be a common thief. We found the squadron leader's wallet on him. It contained five one-pound notes, and some coins were found in his pocket. Any casual thief would have taken the lot."

"Unless he was disturbed."

"An outside possibility, but I think it likely that there was another motive. Grindlethorpe thought somebody was tailing him, perhaps intending to kill him. And, as I said, he mentions a number of names." Ruskin took a drag on his cigarette. "Yours is one of them, as a matter of fact."

"What? But that's ridiculous. Why would I want to kill Grindlethorpe?"

Ruskin looked Gus in the eye. "Flight Lieutenant Beaumont, when did you last see Squadron Leader Grindlethorpe?"

"When he left the library on Thursday. That would be … let me think … just after seven, maybe ten minutes past."

"Did he say where he was going?"

"He said he was working late, till about nine. Then he'd go for a fish supper."

"Do you know where he lived?"

"Somewhere near Regent's Park, I believe."

"Well, Grindlethorpe never got there. The doctor estimates he died between ten p.m. on Thursday and four a.m. the following morning. Can you tell me where you were, and what you were doing, on the night of Thursday the first and Friday the second of October?"

Gus let out a sigh of despair. "I was in London on leave from my base at that time. RAF Tempsford."

"Anyone with you?"

"Yes, my fiancée. Miss Eunice Hesketh."

"Can she corroborate your story?"

"It isn't a story."

"Can your fiancée confirm that you were in London with her?"

"Yes. Well, until I put her on the train at King's Cross, she can."

"What time was that?"

"I saw her off. She took the late train to Edinburgh. It left King's Cross just after ten."

"What did you do afterwards?"

"I walked to Marylebone station…"

"Marylebone? Well, well. That's roughly midway between where Squadron Leader Grindlethorpe worked, on Baker Street, and where he died, isn't it?"

"I don't know where Grindlethorpe was killed. I'm telling you, I walked to Marylebone, then took a train to Eunice's flat in Hampstead. I got there at about eleven. I have a key. I stayed there on Thursday night. The next morning, I was up early. I had to report back for duty at RAF Tempsford."

"So you're saying that you were alone during the time that Grindlethorpe was killed, and spent most of it in your fiancée's flat in Hampstead?"

Gus nodded.

"But there's no one to corroborate this?"

"No."

Detective Inspector Ruskin stubbed what remained of his Senior Service cigarette into the ashtray. "Flight Lieutenant Beaumont, I am…"

The door burst open, and in rushed a red-faced Jimmy James. With him were Group Captain Whitworth, Anderson-Maggs and another RAF police officer, this one a flight lieutenant.

Gus sprung to attention and saluted. Ruskin looked stunned.

"Stop this interview at once," said Whitworth.

"This is Flight Lieutenant John Colson of the Royal Air Force Police, Special Investigation Branch,' Anderson-Maggs said 'I am now handing over to him. Flight Lieutenant, please carry on."

"Thank you, sir. From now on, the investigation into Squadron Leader Grindlethorpe's death will be undertaken by the RAF Police."

"Nonsense," said Ruskin. "This is a civil matter and you know it. A murder took place in London, and Scotland Yard is the proper force to investigate it. You have no jurisdiction, Colson. I informed your people that I intended to come onto this base to interview Flight Lieutenant Beaumont, and your man here, Flying Officer Anderson-Maggs, has been in the building the whole time."

Colson placed a letter on the desk. "Not so, I'm afraid," he said, firmly. "This order is signed by high authority at both the Air Chief Marshal's office and the Home Office. It makes it clear this is a military matter, and I shall personally carry on the investigation." Colson stared at DI Ruskin, then smiled. "It's no longer your case, old boy. Sorry."

CHAPTER 13

Gus left Jimmy's office and found that a letter had arrived from Eunice. Gus took it from the mess and dashed up to his room to read it.

Dear Gus,

Thank you for your letter — all is well here. As well as can be expected. It's difficult not being able to tell Duncan's parents everything, of course. No, I'm not too cold.

How did dinner in the French officers' mess go? I hope you didn't dribble your soup, or anything ghastly!

Yes, I did read about Grindlethorpe. How awful.

Sorry to hear of your bad news, but I'm sure it will only be for a short while.

The wedding preparations are going splendidly. That is what you still want, isn't it? For us to be married?

I'm afraid your other questions took me a bit by surprise, really. Our future together once we're wed? Starting a family straight away? Where to live?

Gus, there's a war on! Until it's all over, we can't make plans like that.

I'd thought that after the wedding, and possibly a brief honeymoon, if we're lucky, we'd both go back to our jobs until the war is over.

I miss you very much and look forward to you coming up to Edinburgh when you can get away. Hope that will be soon.

Your dearest, ever-loving Eunice XX

SWALK

Later, Commandant Pascal Pascale stood before the officers of Thiès Squadron in their briefing room. Beside him was the squadron's intelligence officer, Capitaine Laroche, a middle-aged, balding man with a handlebar moustache. As liaison officer, Gus was there as part of the assembled throng. Diplomatically, he'd decided to sit at the back of the room.

A piece of paper in his right hand, Pascale addressed his officers. "Gentlemen, I have here a note from Air Chief Marshal Harris. As you know, he is the commander-in-chief of RAF Bomber Command. This is what he writes, and my thanks to Flight Lieutenant Beaumont for the excellent translation." He began to read aloud. *"Today your squadron will become operational for the first time, actively participating in the liberation of your country. You represent the glorious fighting spirit of France. I wish you luck."*

There was applause from the officers, but Pascale raised a hand.

"It isn't time to congratulate ourselves yet. When we return, perhaps. Tonight, our target will be the Rhine city of Düsseldorf. I'll now hand over to Capitaine Laroche."

A sense of excitement overtook the room as Laroche began, "The RAF Pathfinders have adopted a number of new techniques. Their force is split into three groups for this raid. First, a small flight of so-called 'illuminators' will drop white target flares along the attack vector pathway. Next, coloured indicators will be dropped on the target itself, followed by the 'fire starters', who will use those flares as the aim point for their incendiaries. Of course, the incendiaries will burn longer than any flares and it is these you are to aim at.

"These new techniques were first employed last month on a raid of two hundred and fifty-one aircraft against Bremen. It was highly successful. The post-raid analysis showed that hundreds of light and medium industrial buildings, including the Weser aircraft works and the Atlas shipyard and associated warehouses were destroyed. They also hit four hundred and sixty houses, which were destroyed. A further one and a half thousand houses were seriously damaged. It seems, gentlemen, the new tactics were a complete success.

"Tonight, the Pathfinders will lead a combined attack by almost five hundred aircraft. Here is the route." With a stick, he pointed to the arrows on the map. "We take off at 1130 and assemble over the mouth of the Humber, north of Grimsby at ten thousand feet. Then it's south-east; the precise magnetic bearings are here." He waved a piece of paper.

"I'll pin this up and the navigators can copy them down afterwards. As you can see on the map, your route clips the coast of Norfolk and crosses the Dutch coast here —" he pointed with his stick — "between Renesse and Domburg. Then we alter course and fly along the attack vector which will, don't forget, be illuminated by white markers. Once the bombs are gone, pull out to starboard and return on a westerly course, over Ghent. Turn north once you are over Dunkirk. British coastal defence batteries have been warned; they won't open fire on you."

His briefing finished, Laroche took a seat and deferred to Pascale. The squadron leader stood. "Now, you bomb-aimers, I don't want to hear of any creep-back. Do not under any circumstances let loose your bombs until you are absolutely sure you're over the target. I trust you all understand."

The officers were silent throughout this briefing. Navigators sat making notes in their logbooks, checking maps, and measuring distances and angles. Nobody wanted to be the one to make a mistake. Nobody wanted to be the one that got their

Stirling bomber and its crew lost before the illuminated vector was visible.

"Any questions?" asked Pascale.

Pierre Soutine was first to raise his hand. "At what altitude do we drop the bombs, sir?"

Pascale turned to Laroche, who replied, "Fifteen thousand feet. You need to be at that height as you cross the German border and maintain it until the bombs are gone."

"Yes?" said Pascale, turning to Capitaine Louis Pinault, whose hand was now raised.

"What's the flak report on the Dutch coast, sir?"

Again, Pascale deferred to Laroche.

"You're crossing the distributary delta of the Rhine. Anti-aircraft batteries are there, but not in any great concentration. Approach at maximum altitude…"

"And hope for the best," came a voice from the rear of the room.

"Who was that?" demanded Pascale, but nobody answered. "Gentlemen, I will not tolerate insubordination amongst my officers. Who made that comment? I demand to know."

The room was silent. There was shuffling in the row in front of Gus. A young officer he did not know got to his feet.

"It was me, Commandant Pascale. I forgot myself for a moment and I apologise profusely, sir."

"I shall see you in my office immediately after this briefing."

"Yes, sir."

"If you are caught by a searchlight," Pascale went on, "you take avoiding action as you have been trained to do. Then you get back on course as quickly as you possibly can. Now, any more questions? No? Then you are dismissed. Good luck, gentlemen."

At 2330 Pierre's crew were driven to their Stirling in a lorry, which stopped under the aircraft's port wing. Izzy Parry drove behind it, with Gus in the passenger seat of the car. She pulled up beside the French crew.

Pierre and his crew clambered out of the lorry and walked towards the door at the rear of the aeroplane. Gus overtook them and stood by the door. He shook hands with each of them and wished them luck as they climbed in. Pierre was the only one to speak. "Thank you for coming to see us off," he said.

"Not at all. What happened to that officer who spoke out of turn?"

"Blanchard? He's been demoted from lieutenant to sous-lieutenant with immediate effect."

"Ouch!"

"He was a fool to say what he did, even though we were all thinking it."

Most of the French airmen gave a smile or a nod, but one of them, Marcel Poincare, rounded on Gus.

"I suppose you're thankful you're not with us tonight, Englishman? Just like Dunkirk, isn't it? You get to safety whilst we French get shot at."

Gus span around to confront the Frenchman. Izzy, who had heard what Poincare said, grasped Gus's sleeve and pulled him back just as he was about to respond.

"Don't say anything," she whispered, shaking her head.

"Why did he have to come out with that?" asked Gus as Izzy drove back towards the control tower.

"It'll be the tension. It builds up, obviously. I've seen it before, and I'm sure he didn't mean any harm."

"Mean any harm? I'll knock his bloody block off if he talks to me like that again."

"Just calm down," she said, gently squeezing his hand.

From the control tower, Gus and Izzy watched as the Stirlings of Thiès Squadron taxied out to the end of the Elvington runway, turned into wind and, one by one, their engines roaring, rolled along the strip and took to the air.

With the last of the bombers airborne, Gus turned to Izzy. "Fancy a cup of tea?"

"Why not?" she said. "The NAAFI will still be open."

"Come on, then. Let's dash over before it closes."

Waiting for the return of a night bomber raiding squadron was never an easy thing to do. Gus and Izzy talked away those tense hours. It turned out that Izzy was the daughter of an office worker at the Milk Marketing Board. She came from Bilton, once a small village and now a suburb of Harrogate, in the foothills of the Yorkshire Dales. Izzy had volunteered for the WAAFs only last year, when she'd turned eighteen; that made her three years younger than Gus. Her basic training was at West Drayton, from where she'd been posted to Elvington. She relished the work, she told him. She'd learned to drive in the WAAF. She had a role that got her out and about, and she'd gained much more independence than she'd ever had back in Bilton.

She wrote to her family every week and had managed to visit Bilton two or three times since she'd been at Elvington. With a cheeky smile, she added that her parents were worried about her wellbeing, with so many young men around the base.

Eventually, Izzy and Gus lapsed into silence, drinking tea, and watching and waiting for the return of the Stirling bombers of Thiès Squadron.

CHAPTER 14

"Listen," said Izzy, "engines."

Gus listened. She was right. He looked at his wristwatch. It was 0415 and he, too, could hear the noise of the engines getting steadily louder.

"Come on," he said. "Let's get down there."

They had gone from the NAAFI canteen back to the control tower. Now, they rushed outside. As they gazed into the darkness, Gus could tell that one of the bombers was in trouble.

"It's coming in with only three engines running."

"Can you see from here?" asked Izzy. "I can only just make out the shape of the plane."

"I can't see, but I can hear. It's an engine down. And one of the others sounds dodgy. Listen."

The Bristol Hercules which powered the Stirling bombers was a bigger, more powerful version of the Bristol Mercury radial engine fitted to the Lysanders. The Mercury had only nine cylinders, whereas the Hercules had fourteen. Gus was used to these engines and was confident he could hear if anything was playing up.

As the Stirling got closer, they could make out the lettering. It was Capitaine Louis Pinault's C for Charles. As far as Gus could see through the darkness, it was in one piece. As he watched, Louis made a fair landing on the three engines, then taxied over to the apron. There, his crew disembarked and a lorry drove them over to the buildings for their debrief.

As the lorry pulled away, Gus and Izzy could hear the roar and occasional stutters of other heavy aircraft beginning to fill the air. There was no point looking on from the apron beside the control tower, so Gus beckoned Izzy and they drove over to the building where Commandant Pascale would meet his crews. Gus went into the debrief building, while Izzy waited with the car.

"How was it, Louis?" Pascale asked the capitaine.

"Not so bad, I suppose, sir," Louis replied between deep drags on a Gitanes cigarette. "We hit flak on the way out — bloody terrifying, but we came through it unscathed. I saw one of our aeroplanes caught in the lights, poor bastards. The approach vector was lit up as planned, and we dropped our bombs over the target. At least, I think we did. The inner port engine overheated on the way home, so I had the flight engineer shut it down. The plane flew fine on the other three, though the outer starboard is sounding ropey."

"You did well. We'll soon have the mechanics looking at your engines," said Pascale. "Let's hear what the others have to say."

Lorries and buses were arriving and bomber crews coming into the debrief building. Gus looked around but couldn't see Pierre Soutine.

"Are all the planes home?" he asked.

"No, sir," replied an NCO flight controller. "Four of them are still out there. Ah, I think I can hear engines now."

Gus rushed to the door and went outside to face the runway. He listened to the engine noise, which he thought lumpy to say the least. At least one, maybe two, of the four engines were damaged in some way or other. The pilot must have been having a difficult time with her.

"Who is it?" he asked a French ground crew member beside him.

"B for *Bravade*, I think. Capitaine Soutine."

It was indeed Pierre Soutine. The Stirling came into view as it approached the landing strip. Pierre glided down and brought the Stirling into its flare, landing at just the right moment. With hardly a bump, the heavy bomber made a three-point touchdown, then taxied to the end of the runway, where it turned.

A bus brought Pierre and his crew to the debrief building. Pierre walked in first. A trickle of dried blood ran down his right cheek, and his uniform was smoke-damaged. Only four out of his six-man air crew were with him.

"What happened?" asked Pascale.

"We were hit by flak on the way over the Dutch coast. We took a hit at the front, starboard side. I lost some of the Perspex and Marcel was wounded. An arm injury — it didn't seem too serious and the plane was handling well, so I decided to carry on. We moved Marcel to the crew rest bunk and Martin Blum, the flight engineer, took the co-pilot controls to help me. For a while, everything was going according to plan. Then, on the run in, we were attacked by a night fighter. A Ju-88. He came out of nowhere, and opened up at close range from underneath. Laval was looking down through the bomb-aimer's window. He didn't stand a chance. I'll write to his family.

"Anyway, I took avoiding action by turning to starboard and corkscrewing the kite. We lost the fighter, but the gunfire damaged the inner port engine. I could see the illuminated target, so I had another run at it from a different direction. We dropped our bombs over the target, sir."

"Well done, Pierre," said Pascale. "We've got another job tonight, so you'd better get some rest. We'll get your Stirling patched up, and I'll have a co-pilot transferred from the reserve pool. No navigators around at the moment, I'm afraid.

But I'll think up something — otherwise, you'll just have to do your best."

"I can navigate, sir," said Gus.

"You?"

"Yes, sir. I'm a pilot, but all of my substantive squadron are also trained navigators. We fly single-handed."

"And what about night navigation?"

"I have plenty of experience, sir. I'll go and fetch my logbook, if you want to see it."

Pascale looked at Pierre Soutine, who nodded.

"I trust you, Gus," said Pierre. "If you tell me you're a qualified navigator with night experience and you're keen to fly with us, then we'll be happy to have you along." He looked to his CO.

"Done," said Pascale. "Now all we have to do is get those engines fixed and the Perspex mended."

Back in his room, Gus tried to sleep, but it was difficult. What had he done? He'd swapped a safe posting as ground-based liaison officer for a damned dangerous one as a night navigator in a Short Stirling bomber. Short by name, short by nature. No wonder they were vulnerable to flak, if they couldn't get above seventeen-thousand feet. At least he wouldn't have to lie in that exposed bomb-aimer's position. He wasn't qualified; another crew member would have to act as bomb-aimer.

His thoughts turned to Izzy. She was a nice, easy-going young woman. He had to admit, he appreciated spending time with her. But what would Eunice think?

Then his thoughts turned to Bunty Kermode. He'd long struggled to decide where she fitted in; then she'd been killed in that blasted German tip-and-run attack.

Was that why he'd volunteered just now? To get back at the Germans? Or was it to prove something to Sous-Lieutenant Marcel Poincare and the other Frenchmen? Poincare was in hospital with a badly broken arm; he wouldn't be around for some time.

As the air crews ate, slept and recovered, Gus knew the ground crews would be getting to work. Riggers would check over airframes and begin their mending. Engineers would service, repair and even replace the damaged engines. The Stirlings would be quickly mended, re-fuelled and loaded up with their mix of high explosive and incendiary bombs, ready for the next mission. *What will it bring?* thought Gus as he closed his eyes.

CHAPTER 15

The next afternoon, Gus attended the briefing alongside Pierre and the replacement co-pilot, Sous-Lieutenant Henri Lacassagne. Afterwards, the three of them were joined by the other officers and Martin Blum, the flight engineer, to discuss all aspects of the mission ahead.

"I don't understand why we're crossing the Dutch coast at our maximum altitude when we know it's too low to avoid the German ack-ack," said Gus.

"We have no alternative; we can't get any higher."

"I understand that. But as we can't get any higher, why not go in lower? Why not cross the Dutch coast at a low level? Approach at, say, two hundred feet and the enemy radar won't pick us up. Climb to fifteen hundred once over the Netherlands and maintain that altitude for the actual bombing approach and release. Granted, it won't protect us from flak closer to the target, but at least we're more likely to arrive there in one piece."

"He's got a point," said Xavier Monet. "We could go in under the radar. The whole attacking force should do that."

"Impossible," said Pierre.

"Why is it impossible?"

"Numbers. There are hundreds of aircraft involved, remember? It would be chaos."

"I agree, up to a point," said Gus. "Yes, it would be impossible with the whole group. There are simply far too many planes to fly in formation at such low altitude. A lone bomber or even a flight of Stirlings could do it, though. The entire Thiès Squadron could probably manage it."

*

After eating and changing into his combat uniform, Gus surveyed the compass and torch he'd bought just the other day. Should he take them along? *Why not?* he thought and shoved them into his pockets.

The seven-man crew were driven by lorry to Stirling B for *Bravade*, which was parked on the apron perimeter. Gus was third up the steps and into the door at the rear port side after Pierre and Henri. He followed them along the rear fuselage walkway to the middle of the plane, through the door into the forward section and took his place at the navigator's table. The pilot and co-pilot ahead of him took their seats on the flight deck. Behind him were Aspirant Xavier Monet the wireless operator and Adjutant Martin Blum, who would undertake the bomb-aimer duties in addition to being flight engineer. Robert Assous and François Le Blanc took up their usual positions at the mid-upper and rear gun turrets.

Pierre started the Stirling's engines one by one. As he did so, the noise inside the aircraft grew louder, far louder than anything Gus had encountered as a pilot. Slowly, the giant beast began to move, taxiing to its place in the queue of bombers making ready to leave Elvington.

"Seats for take-off," ordered Pierre over the RT. "Strap in tight."

The Stirling began to move along the runway. Pierre opened up the throttles, using more port than starboard to counter the prop torque, applying rudder as the speed increased. By now the noise was deafening. Gus felt the tail lifting as the Stirling gained yet more momentum. Now the Stirling was careering down the strip, and Gus felt the sensation of lift as Pierre brought the large aeroplane up into the night sky.

"Undercarriage up, Henri."

"Yes," said the co-pilot, bringing up the landing gear.

They circled over the Humber to form up with the rest of the squadron, then changed course to fly over the North Sea, close to the coast of Norfolk.

"Give me a course to steer, Gus," said Pierre as they cleared Great Yarmouth.

"One-two-five magnetic, Skipper."

"ETA over the Dutch coast?"

"Twenty-four minutes exactly. That's 0130 hours."

"Tell me when we are halfway. We're going to descend to sea level. Let's find out if you are right about avoiding the flak," said Pierre. "Get up into the front turret, Xavier. We'll give the bastards a strafing as we go over the coast."

"Right away," said Xavier, smiling as he left the wireless station and clambered into the front turret, which was armed with two Browning machine guns.

Gus looked out of the port window by his navigator's table as Pierre brought the Stirling down, levelling off two hundred feet above the North Sea. All he could see was water — cold, black water.

"Coast ahead," announced Xavier.

Gus strained to look forward from the side window, but he could see little.

"Ah," said Pierre, "another advantage. From this height, we can actually see the distributaries of the Rhine. I'm going to fly her right up the middle of that one." He pointed out the way ahead to his co-pilot.

Gus saw land out to port as Pierre followed the slightly meandering estuary.

"Ships in the water, Capitaine," called Xavier. "Permission to open fire?"

"Permission granted. François, be ready to spray them as they come into view."

"Yes, sir."

The machine guns at the front of the Stirling opened fire, soon followed by the four in the tail-end turret.

"I've hit one," called François from the rear turret. "I can see flames coming from one of the vessels."

"No, you didn't. It was me that got him," insisted Xavier.

Soon, Pierre began to climb up to a more conventional height. "Xavier, up to the wireless station now. Gus, give me a course to target."

Gus had worked out that Pierre's route had taken them over the Waal, south of both Rotterdam and The Hague. He could make out an island and two bridges. *That must be Dordrecht away to port.* He looked at his map. The target was Duisburg, north of Düsseldorf.

"Course to steer is magnetic one-one-zero. ETA to target twenty minutes."

"Roger. Martin, in ten minutes you need to get down into the bomb-aimer's position. Do any checks you need before that. Understand?"

"Understood, Capitaine. All engine and hydraulic checks done. I'm ready, sir."

From the Stirling's cockpit, Gus and the others looked down on the white target illuminators. Then came the coloured target indicators and, eventually, the bright flames of hundreds of incendiary bombs that lit the target.

The adjutant had left his cockpit position behind the pilots and was at the bomb-aimer's station. Gus could picture him; he'd be forward-facing, lying prone on his belly, and looking down through the sights. His calm voice came over the RT.

"Left, right, right. Steady, steady. Left, steady. Steady, bombs away."

Pierre heaved the Stirling to starboard. "Course for home, Gus, please?"

"Two-seventy degrees, magnetic. Due west, Skipper. That will take us to the coast at Flushing."

"Take the controls, Henri. Martin, good work. Get back up here, will you? Xavier, Robert and François, keep a good look out for night fighters."

"Yes, Capitaine."

Pierre came over to crouch beside Gus and look at the map. "Show me where we went."

Gus pointed out the route they had followed at low level along the river Waal distributary.

"It worked out very well," said Pierre. "We could share it with the others, hear their views. If we do that, however, it may well bring a reprimand from Comandante Pascale. I'm not sure what to do."

"And we know it isn't a viable tactic in large numbers," added Gus.

"Correct. Perhaps we'll keep it to ourselves."

"I suppose so."

The remainder of the return flight was almost uneventful. They crossed the coast at Flushing as Gus said they would, encountering a smattering of German flak. Then they crossed the North Sea and hit some low cloud as they crossed the English coast. Elvington was sighted and Pierre called them into their seats for the descent, then brought B for *Bravade* down for another near-perfect landing back at base.

After debriefing, hot drinks and sandwiches, Gus and the other crew members went off to their rooms to get some sleep. Gus was dreading it.

CHAPTER 16

Gus felt that he needed a break from the French crew. Trying to be constantly diplomatic whilst feeling tested was wearing him down. Over the next few days, he found himself spending more time in the British officers' mess. One morning, he sat drinking tea with Jimmy James and David Barnes. Around them were a score of other officers; noise and cigarette smoke enveloped them all.

"How's it going with the Frenchmen, Bouncer?" asked Jimmy, stirring yet more sugar into his tea.

"Not bad, not bad at all."

"They seem to have settled in well enough."

"Yes. Everyone agrees they've settled in well."

"I hear a few of them went into York the other day," said David.

"Yes. That didn't go so well, I'm afraid," Gus replied with a sigh.

"Oh. Why not?"

"They couldn't find anywhere selling white wine, so they tried beer. Hated it."

"Ha! Don't blame them. This bloody weak-as-water Yorkshire ale. Can't beat a pint of Kentish bitter, in my opinion."

"I expect they'll get used to it," said David. "Are they still complaining about their Stirlings?"

"Of course they are. You know what they're like."

David laughed. "They'll get used to them too, eventually. Just give it time." He ground the stub of his Capstan into the pewter ashtray.

"I'm not sure I'll ever get used to it all, though," said Gus.

"It was good of you to step up like that," said David. "To go with them as a navigator. Must be different from flying single-engined kites around, but you'll settle into it too, I expect."

"It's not that," said Gus.

Jimmy looked at him knowingly. "Any more news about that other stuff, Bouncer? You know, the murder and all? I expect that's getting you down."

"No news. Heard nothing more about it. You're right, though. It does play on my mind, being a suspect, you know?"

"Forget it. I would," said Jimmy. "It's not easy, but it's the best way."

"It's not being under suspicion that's bothering me. And it's not going up with the French. I don't mind that at all. No, it's the bombing itself. You know what I mean? The very idea of it. I…" He faltered, picked up his cup and took a sip of tea before carrying on. "I just don't like the idea of it. If I'm honest, I think I detest it. It seems too much like … like murder to me."

Jimmy glared at Gus. A deep frown scarred his forehead. "Not sure I do know what you mean, old man, as a matter of fact," he said. "The Air Marshal says it's essential that we knock out Jerry's infrastructure. His factories, roads, railways. His docks and bridges. All the bloody lot. If some civvies get caught up around the edges of it, well, that's just their bad luck. It's orders. That's what Bomber Harris says, and that's what we're doing."

Gus opened his mouth to respond but was interrupted by David Barnes.

"Come off it, Jimmy. You know as well as we all do that it's not about getting caught around the edges. Most of our bombs miss. There was a raid on Hamburg the other week —

afterwards, our photographers worked out that only twenty per cent of the bombs hit the intended target. Where do you think the rest landed? Goodness knows how many poor bloody civilians get killed in the average raid. Thousands, I should think. And as for calling the Air Marshal 'Bomber' Harris — that's just what the papers call him. 'Butcher' Harris is more accurate. That's what the bomber crews call him."

Having finished talking, David sat puffing on a cigarette and staring into his teacup. Gus looked at the young pilot. He was ashen-faced, with bags under his eyes. *My God*, thought Gus. *This bloody war is having a bad effect on all of us.* But he had to concur with David.

"He's absolutely right," agreed Gus. "We're aiming for Jerry's infrastructure, sure. We might tell ourselves we're bombing accurately and hitting it. But we're kidding ourselves. Oh yes, we might well hit the targets — sometimes. We're almost bound to, with the amount of high explosive and incendiary bombs we drop. But we're also destroying homes. Hitting families — women and children. Killing and maiming them, and causing goodness knows what scars in the minds of survivors. We know we are."

"It's no bloody different to what the Germans did to our cities in the Blitz," Jimmy insisted. "It's just the bloody same, isn't it?"

"Does that make it right?" asked David.

Jimmy banged his teacup onto the table. Tea spilled over his hand. "It was the bloody Germans that started it in the first place, wasn't it?" Jimmy was shouting now.

The background noise of the mess suddenly stopped. All eyes turned towards Jimmy.

"Yes, but…"

"Yes, but nothing!" yelled Jimmy, rising from his seat. "I've had enough of this talk. All was well here till you arrived, Beaumont!" He rounded on Gus, jabbing a finger at him.

Gus rose and opened his mouth to defend himself. David held him back.

"I didn't know we had bloody pacifists in the camp!" barked Jimmy.

"I'm not a bloody pacifist!" shouted Gus.

"Leave it, Bouncer," said David as Jimmy stormed out of the mess, slamming the door shut after him. "It's nothing to do with you being posted here, and Jimmy knows that. Some of us have been pondering the morality of what we do. But it does no good in the long run."

Gus sat down. "What do you mean?"

"I mean we can't change it."

"I suppose not."

"Any one of us could refuse to go out there. If we did, we'd be up before a court martial. Any one of us could go to the doc and feign an illness to get out of a raid, but we'd be letting our comrades down."

Gus nodded his reluctant agreement.

"So, we just get on with it. If I'm honest, I think most of us try our damned hardest to do our jobs well, to hit the targets. Creep-back is an issue, sure it is. But I don't think it's deliberate. Survival instinct kicks in up there. Command is doing what it can with these improved Pathfinder tactics." David paused to take a sip of tea. "And, most of all, Bouncer old man, it's a bloody war. We're in it and we just have to do our best to get through it and hold our heads up afterwards."

"You're right, David. It's hard to take, knowing what we're doing, but you're right. There's a war on, as people say."

"Yes. And ugly things happen in wars."

Later, alone in his room, Gus considered recent events. What a bloody mess. What was Jimmy's outburst all about? Wasn't it reasonable to discuss the basis on which they acted out this bloody war? Perhaps not. Gus was sorry he'd brought it up.

Gus looked at his hands. They were shaking. He'd developed a twitch below his right eye that wouldn't go away. He needed to rest.

Perhaps, he thought at last, when once again sleep wouldn't come, perhaps he needed to see a doctor.

PART TWO: NOVEMBER 1942

CHAPTER 17

A couple of days' leave, thought Gus, as he pulled himself out of the single bed in his room in the British officers' mess. *What a bloody luxury, and I think I need it.* He looked at the time. He needed to get a move on.

Two days before, Gus had received a letter from his cousin, Staś Rosen. The sombre tone of the missive troubled him. His cousin seemed to be in a dark place.

Gus had suggested they meet, and they'd settled on Peterborough as a rendezvous. Neither of them knew the town, but it was easy for Gus to travel to and not too far out of London for Staś.

After a rushed breakfast in the mess, Izzy Parry drove Gus to York station. He picked up a newspaper and caught a fast train bound for London. The train was busy, and Gus found it difficult to find a seat, but at least it steamed quickly south from Yorkshire and into the East Midlands.

He looked at the front page of the paper he'd picked up at the station. It covered a more detailed analysis of the US Navy's victory over the Japanese in the Battle of Cape Esperance the previous month. Gus turned to the inner pages and read that Hitler had ordered captured Allied commandos to be killed. *The bastard's rattled*, he thought. Perhaps Dieppe and the other Combined Ops raids were making a difference after all.

Reading the newspaper helped pass the time. Gus half-heartedly attempted the crossword puzzle, though he'd never been much good at them. He just couldn't get the hang of the cryptic clues. Soon the express was slowing down on its approach to Peterborough station. Gus put his paper away and went out of the compartment and into the crowded passageway where people were standing. The train came to a halt, and he clambered down from the carriage, spotting Staś wating for him on the platform.

Gus had thought his cousin would be pleased to see him, but Staś did not look at all happy. He looked like a man with the weight of the world upon his young shoulders.

As the two shook hands, Gus noticed that his cousin's grip, usually so firm, was weak. "What on earth is wrong?" he demanded.

"It's Butch Paderewski," said Staś. "He's dead."

Butch was a colleague and mutual friend of theirs. A US citizen of Polish descent from Krakow, Wisconsin, he had been a very good fighter pilot.

"Butch? Oh no! That is bad news," Gus said sadly. "Look, let's pop over to the buffet and see if we can get a drink. You can tell me all about it."

"What time is it?" asked Staś.

"Half past eleven. The bar will be open."

"I need to be back by three."

They walked over to the bar in Peterborough station. Gus sat Staś down and went to order. "Two Scotches, make them double. Just a cube of ice with each," he told the barmaid. She looked at him oddly, clearly surprised that he was ordering spirits so early in the day, but she made no comment and served the drinks. Gus paid and walked back to where Staś was sitting.

He passed one of the glasses to his cousin. "Cheers. Now, tell me what happened."

"Cheers." Staś clinked glasses with Gus and took a swig of the fiery spirit. "Butch was hit by a train. He was killed instantly."

"What? How?"

"He was on the track, Gus. Butch was walking on the track."

"You mean he…"

"We don't know. Not for sure, but…" Staś took another drink, emptying his glass. "Butch had been suffering. He'd lost a lot of comrades. Friends. You know what it's like."

"Yes, I know," agreed Gus. The Polish squadron had suffered many casualties. He still grieved for Tunio Nowacki.

"He was tormented — we could all see that. Had been for months. Things started to go wrong, little things at first. He'd forget to hand in a report, forget his Mae West. Once, he almost landed with the undercarriage up and had to pull out at the last second and go around again. Eventually, Butch was grounded following a bad landing incident. He taxied in front of a Spitfire and caused the pilot to pull out left at low altitude. He collided with some trees. We lost the pilot and the Spit. Entirely Butch's fault — he acknowledged that. Two days later, he was hit by that train. He was wearing his dog-tags, so at least we didn't have to go to the mortuary and identify what was left of him." Staś looked away, and Gus saw the horror on his cousin's face. "But that's not the end of the matter. There's an inquest going on right now. They're trying to say it was suicide."

"Was it?"

"Who knows? He didn't leave a note. He didn't talk about ending his life. Butch seemed to be existing in a daze. Shell-shocked — that's what they would have said in the last war, I guess. He might have simply wandered onto the track, the state of mind he was in."

"Maybe."

"Here's the worst part of it, Gus. If the inquest finds Butch took his own life, there's no pension for his wife. That's what the Ministry is up to, trying to save money. Disgusting!"

Gus looked at Staś. His cousin's eyes were watery. *This is what war does to us*, thought Gus. *It robs brave men of their friends and their dignity.* "Come on, Staś," he said. "We'll get another drink, then some food."

The thought of Butch Paderewski's body lying crushed and mangled on a railway track bothered Gus all the way back to York. He tried to visualise the scene, then stopped. The very idea that the British authorities were penny-pinching to the extent that they would try to prove Butch's death was suicide concerned him deeply, but he tried to put the matter out of his mind. Instead, he turned his attention to his fiancée, but no matter how hard he tried, Gus found no solace there.

What was happening? His feelings for Eunice seemed to be somehow weakening. He tried to doze off, but hadn't managed it by the time the train was pulling into York station.

Outside the station, Izzy Parry was waiting for him with a car. "We'll soon have you back at base, Mr Beaumont," she said, cheerily.

"No," he blurted. "Let's go somewhere for a drink, shall we?"

"If you like," she smiled.

Izzy drove through the darkness of York city centre. Instead of taking the usual route to Elvington, she diverted towards Heslington and, once in the village, stopped and parked the car by a village pub.

"Will this do us?" she asked, pulling on the handbrake and switching off the engine.

"Perfect," he said with a heavy sigh.

"Blimey, you sound as though you've had a bad day."

"I have," he said, looking into her eyes, "but it's getting better by the minute."

She met his gaze, smiling. "Come on. Let's have that drink."

CHAPTER 18

A few days later, Commandant Pascal Pascale stood before his officers once more. Gus was present, a replacement navigator not having yet arrived. It was another briefing before yet another raid. Beside Pascale, as usual, was Capitaine Laroche, the squadron's intelligence officer. This time, Laroche had photographs, which clearly showed that their raid on Duisburg had failed to find its target.

Pascale addressed his officers. "Gentlemen, our raid last week didn't have as much success as we had anticipated. Our target tonight will be the same again: Duisburg."

Laroche took up the narrative. "Same tactics as before. The 'illuminators' will drop white target flares along the attack vector. The 'visual markers' will drop coloured indicators on the target itself and the 'fire starters' will use the flares as the aiming point for their incendiaries.

"We take off at midnight and assemble, as usual, over the mouth of the Humber. Angels one-zero — from there you navigators know the route."

"Creep-back was the issue last time," said Pascale, joining in, "so don't drop your bombs until you are absolutely sure you are over the target. Any questions?"

There were none.

Afterwards, Pierre gathered his crew together. "I think we should take the same route in as last time," he said. "Low level over the sea and follow the Waal distributary. You can make a plan this time, Gus."

"Wilco."

"Right," Pierre went on, "you've got two hours, men. Meet for the pick-up lorry at 1130 hours."

When it came, the pick-up vehicle was a bus, not a lorry. The French aircrew spread themselves out, one to each two-seater couch.

"This is luxury," said Xavier.

"Make the most of it. You'll be in that front gun turret sooner than you think," laughed Henri Lacassagne, the replacement second pilot.

"Look at François," said Martin Blum. "Tail-end Charlie up in the air and he can't resist it. He's laid out there on the back seat. Look at the bugger!"

"Be quiet!" shouted François. "Can't you see I'm asleep?"

In this manner, the Free French crew joked and laughed their way to their bomber. It was bravado, Gus knew. Each of them put on a front to disguise their fear.

The flight over the North Sea was uneventful. Gus's route and Pierre's pilotage took the Stirling into the mouth of the Waal estuary with the rest of the squadron, but at lower level. The searchlights and light flak along the coast were aimed much higher than the Stirling, but there was always the chance of catching a stray shell. B for *Bravade*'s gunners fired cursory salvos at the lights. François thought he'd put one out.

"Save your ammo," said Henri over the RT.

As Pierre put the bomber into the target approach vector, Adjutant Martin Blum went forward into the bomb-aimer's station in the nose of the Stirling.

This was perhaps the point in the operation where the bomber was at its most vulnerable, thought Gus. The pilot was intent on keeping the Stirling straight and level, responding to his bomb-aimer's instructions with tiny movements of the stick, carefully adjusting the trim of the aeroplane.

"Left. Right, right," said Martin. "Steady, steady … arrrgh!"

Gus started at the sound of machine-gun bullets and shattering Perspex. Then he heard the screams of a man in agony coming from the cockpit.

"Personnel and equipment check," called an agitated voice over the RT. It was the co-pilot, Henri, not Pierre. Gus and all three gunners replied that all was good. Nothing came from the bomb-aimer.

"Fire check?"

Gus looked at the engineer's panel. "Nothing indicated. No smoke."

"We've got to dump these bombs. Martin, are you all right?" the co-pilot called over the RT.

"I'm hit," replied a weak voice.

"Ditch the bloody bombs!"

"St-steady, steady, b-bombs away," Martin managed.

"Xavier, go down and check on him," said Henri, pulling the Stirling to starboard and taking up a westerly course that he knew would lead towards the Dutch coast.

"Corkscrew the bloody plane!" shouted Gus as he made his way to the front of the cockpit. "That night fighter may come back for a second go at us."

"Gus, come up here and help me get the capitaine out of his seat!"

As Henri manoeuvred the gigantic aeroplane into a series of port-starboard turns, losing height as he did so, Gus clambered as quickly as he could to the steps. He was being flung around and tried to keep a tight hold of anything sturdy in order to prevent himself from being tossed to the floor. Eventually he shoved his head up onto the flight deck.

Cold night air blasted into the cockpit, hitting him in the face. Gus saw that a hail of machine-gun bullets had shattered the port side Perspex of the flight deck cockpit. And there was blood, lots of blood. He saw immediately that Pierre was badly hurt. He had slumped forward in his seat, blood already having seeped through his clothing at the back.

Henri levelled the Stirling and got her back on a course for home. The wind in the cockpit was vicious, but with the co-pilot's help, Pierre was moved and passed back. Gus checked him over. There were no signs of life.

Meanwhile, Xavier, the young aspirant, helped a wounded Martin Blum onto the crew rest bunk sandwiched between the wing roots. Once Xavier had returned to the flight deck, he helped Gus move Pierre's body into the dinghy storage area.

"Xavier, go back to the front guns," ordered Henri. "Gus, up here, please."

Gus climbed up into the cockpit.

"I'll take Pierre's place," said Henri. "You come here into the co-pilot's seat. I'll talk you through the main controls."

The Stirling was steady now, flying a course due west.

"Take the control," said Henri. "Get the feel of her. I'll go check on Martin."

Gus tried the controls, changing course, tentatively at first then more confidently. The Stirling was remarkably light for its size. A shallow dive, a steeper climb. He looked at the compass — back on course. Ahead was the coast, but what coast exactly?

Henri returned and took over. "I need a position," he said to Gus.

"Righto, give me a couple of minutes."

Gus went down the steps to the flight deck, grabbed the sextant off the navigating table, then climbed up and put his head into the astrodome. He took two bearings; they were over the coast, so two would be good enough. He sped back to the table, looked at the map and used his plotter. They were more or less over Flushing. Good.

"We're over the Dutch coast. Course to steer is three-two-five magnetic," he announced, then clambered back to the cockpit.

"Xavier, back onto the wireless," ordered Henri. "I'll need you listening soon."

Xavier changed position immediately, leaving the front gun turret unmanned.

The course of three-two-five took the Stirling in a direct line from the Dutch coast at Flushing and over the North Sea. Soon Gus, back in the co-pilot's seat, could see the English coast.

"That's East Anglia, Harwich," he said over the RT. "Steady on this course, and we'll be back in Elvington in no time at all."

Then they saw lights below — searchlights. Flak began exploding around them. It was coming up at them from Harwich.

"It's our own bloody gunners," said Gus.

"Has nobody warned the British crews at Harwich about us?"

If they had been forewarned, perhaps some army gunners hadn't got the message. Or maybe somebody had itchy fingers. Whatever the cause, Stirling B for *Bravade* was under attack from friendly flak.

An explosion close to the front port section of the plane jolted the Stirling violently. Gus saw holes in the Perspex opposite him. Exploded shell casing had penetrated the cockpit. He looked at Henri. He was slumped forward. A piece of smouldering metal protruded from the pilot's back, dark red blood oozing from the wound. He leant over, shaking Henri by the shoulder and calling his name. Then he took a closer look at the co-pilot. The right-hand side of his face was missing. He took his wrist and felt for a pulse. Nothing.

Gus instantly grabbed the control stick and pushed his left foot on the rudder bar, trying to regain control. Another blast struck the underbelly of the plane. Gus could see they hadn't been caught in a searchlight beam. It was simply bad luck. A third blast jarred the tail of the Stirling and François Le Blanc's screams sounded over the RT.

"Crew check. Now!" shouted Gus. Only Robert, the upper mid-gunner, and the wireless operator, Xavier, responded.

"Robert, I'm taking command," said Gus over the RT. "Go to the rear and check on François."

"Yes, sir."

Moments later, Robert's voice returned. "François is gone, Capitaine."

Pierre, Henri and François were dead. Blum, the flight engineer, lay wounded on the crew bunk.

Gus was now flying over The Wash and thinking about how he was going to land the Stirling.

"Robert," he called, "talk to the flight engineer. Find out as much about landing this monster as you can, then get back up here. Xavier, get on the wireless and listen for the radio beam. Fifteen minutes to landing."

Wind was forecast from the east. That meant Gus flying out towards industrial west Yorkshire and turning once he judged the line of approach back to Elvington would run directly into wind. From then on, he would lose height following the directions called out by the young wireless operator. It didn't matter that Xavier was only nineteen, he reminded himself. He was as experienced as any of them. When should he get the wheels down? What was the stall speed of the Stirling? What advice had the wounded flight engineer managed to convey to Robert?

As Gus was considering all of this, Robert pushed his head up into the cockpit.

"What did Blum tell you?"

"He just said these planes have a nasty habit of stalling over the runway and landing heavily. If that happens, the undercarriage is likely to break."

"Thanks," said Gus. That was all he needed.

The Stirling came into wind four miles west of Elvington. Gus kept his eyes on the altimeter as he throttled off all engines.

"Xavier and Robert," said Gus over the RT, "make sure Martin is strapped securely onto the bunk. Once I can see the strip, you two are going to bail out. Understand?"

"No, we shall stay with you," said Xavier.

"Listen," said Gus, as confidently as he could, "I am the senior officer here, and I am in command. Aspirant Monet and Adjutant Assous, you are to ensure that Adjutant Blum is safely strapped onto his bunk. Then you are both to put on your parachutes. When I give the order, you will exit the aircraft by means of the ventral escape hatch. Any delay will threaten this aircraft and others. That is an order. Is it clear?"

"Yes, sir," they replied.

As they progressed, Xavier's voice guided Gus via the RT. "Left, right, right, steady. Right, right, left a little."

"I can see the strip now," said Gus. "Bail, bail! Out you go!"

Gus was worried they might be too low, but thankfully he saw the two parachutes open and drift down to earth. They might have a bumpy landing, but at least two of the crew would be safe. He pulled on the hydraulic switch gear which lowered the undercarriage as the Stirling approached the

Elvington landing strip. Then he flared out for landing, bringing the Stirling's nose up slightly.

The bomber suddenly began to stall, and Gus felt her drop like a stone towards the runway. With such a heavy aircraft, Gus knew that a dropped landing could cause serious structural damage. Instinctively, he opened up all four throttles simultaneously to compensate, but this caused the aircraft to swing violently to the right. The Stirling became uncontrollable. The starboard wheel touched down heavily, collapsing the landing gear. A great screeching sound was accompanied by a light shower of sparks as the starboard wing touched down. This was quickly followed by the underbelly of the Stirling, which was now pirouetting anticlockwise as it careered along the Elvington strip.

Thank the Lord we were not loaded with bombs and fuel, thought Gus as the heavy bomber finally came to a stop.

Fire crews were there in no time. Gus unstrapped and descended to the flight deck to check on Blum, the flight engineer. He was breathing. Gus ran back to the steps which led up to the cabin roof escape hatch, forcing the door open. "Here, here!" he shouted. "Badly wounded man inside."

Gus clambered onto the roof, jumped down onto the port wing and from that onto the ground. He could now leave everything to the emergency team and ground crew. He wiped sweat from his brow and walked over to the ground transport.

In the truck that took Gus and the crew from another bomber across the base, there was silence. In the office he made his report, for what it was worth, then trudged back to his room in the mess.

Lying on his small bed, he thought about how lucky he'd been to survive. Then his thoughts darkened. When would this war be over?

CHAPTER 19

Gus spent the weekend with Izzy.

It was almost bound to happen, he thought. Two lonely people caught up in a war, in events they had absolutely no control over. Him, troubled and exhausted by the tensions of night flying and battle; persecuted by an uncurable insomnia that was wearing him down.

Her? He confessed to himself that he didn't have a clue what motivated Izzy to want him. But then, he had never been the best at understanding women.

She had told Gus that her parents were going to be away for a while. Her uncle was dying, and they were going over to Ormskirk to stay with the family for a few days. Izzy had the keys to their place in Bilton. Why didn't they travel over there, since they both had the weekend off? Gus agreed, telling himself it was innocent enough.

They went by train on Saturday morning and enjoyed a pleasant day in Harrogate. They walked around the park and the nineteenth-century pump room, originally built by the Victorians. Many of the town's large hotels were now the home of government offices that had been moved here from London.

They found a café and had lunch.

Once back at Izzy's parents' house in Bilton, Gus got a fire going and they had tea beside it, listening to the wireless.

"Why are we here?" he asked.

"Because of the war, silly! It mixes things up. Stirs up people, too. People like me wouldn't be going around with people like you if it wasn't for the war, would we?"

"What do you mean, people like me?"

"Refined people. Well educated people, with posh accents." Izzy smiled.

He nodded. She was right, but Gus knew there was something else.

"And," she added, "although the war's brought misery, you know death, destruction and those bloody ration cards; it's brought excitement too!"

Izzy was right, he thought. The war was a dreadful, appalling thing, but it had its moments of excitement. Real, adrenaline-fuelled exhilaration. Elation up there in the wide, blue yonder. Or here down on the ground. Here with Izzy Parry, perhaps.

"And who knows what tomorrow will bring," he added.

"Who knows?"

"When you looked me in the eye the other night, you smiled," he reminded her.

"I did."

"Why?"

"Because of what I saw in your eyes. Or what I thought I saw."

"What did you see?"

She hesitated. "An interest in me. Desire, maybe," she said, blushing slightly. "Look, I'm sorry if I got it wrong, if I misunderstood…"

Gus took hold of her hand. There was no resistance. "You didn't get it wrong." He moved closer to her, held her slender body in his arms and kissed her. Their first caresses were soft, but soon became firmer; ardent.

Suddenly he stopped and moved away from her, looking her in the eye with a seriousness the moment seemed not to warrant. "Are you sure you want to do this, Izzy?"

"Yes, Gus. I'm absolutely sure."

When it happened, their lovemaking was as passionate as it was sensual, as healing as it was urgent.

Afterwards, although his body was spent and relaxed, Gus struggled to sleep. His mind was elsewhere. Active. Too active. This was part of the problem — whatever he did, he just could not stop thinking.

He was attracted to Izzy, but why? How much of it was simply her easy-going, youthful charm? It was all of that. But there was something else, too. He felt a distinct sense of excitement whenever he was with her. He'd never experienced the same thing with Eunice, nor Bunty, for that matter. Did this excitement come from the fact that their association was at least slightly illicit, because of the difference in their ranks? Very likely, he supposed.

On the other hand, Gus knew he had no deeper feelings for this young woman. Was he taking advantage of her? No. They were both adults and had their eyes open. But he had to admit, their view might be tainted by the proximity of the war. *For God's sake*, he thought, *we might not make it to next week.*

No, he was not in love with Izzy. And Eunice? Gus was disturbed to realise that his feelings for his fiancée had faded.

What had he got himself into? Proposing marriage to Eunice in the middle of a bloody war? Was that sensible? No, he might be dead within twenty-four hours. He tried to take stock of the situation. He'd lost both his parents and many friends and comrades over the last three years. Recently, he'd found out that a close friend had probably committed suicide. He'd very nearly died the other night in that deathtrap of a Stirling bomber. After all, most of the crew were casualties of that last operation. To top it all, he was still, as far as he knew, a suspect in a murder enquiry.

And now his love for Eunice seemed to have disappeared. He had to write to her. He had to end their engagement.

Sunday's weather was as grey as the mood Gus found himself in. He knew it wasn't easy for civilians because of rationing, but he was still surprised by the lack of food in the Parrys' larder. Izzy cooked them a breakfast of mushrooms, rabbit liver and toast made from a 'national loaf' of wholemeal bread.

"This bloody bread is revolting, don't you think?"

"You're too fussy, Gus. Just eat it up."

That is one of the differences between us, he thought. *Izzy has probably been brought up on food not much better than this. I was used to a much finer diet prior to the war.*

In that instant he realised it wasn't going to work out, Izzy and him. There was certainly a mutual attraction, but it would have been better to have kept it at a friendly level. *I've made a mistake,* he thought.

In the afternoon they walked through the rain to Harrogate station and sat holding hands on the journey back to York.

"Had a nice weekend, love?" she asked.

Izzy flinched as he relaxed his hold on her hand. She hadn't meant anything more than a cozy familiarity when she'd addressed Gus as 'love'. It was Yorkshire speak, nothing more.

Yet the word had hit Gus as hard as a blow to the chin. He struggled to know his own feelings.

"Yes," he replied. "You?"

"Wonderful. Thanks ever so much."

They parted outside the base with a hug and a kiss on the cheek, but it felt rather forced after their night of ardour.

Once he was back on base, Gus needed a drink, but something told him not to go to the mess. Instead, he rushed to his room, where he knew he had half a bottle of Scotch. He poured himself a double measure and gulped it back.

Then he searched through the small drawer in which he stored paper and pen, alongside what few valuables he kept with him when in mess: his father's pocket watch, diamond cufflinks and a matching tiepin. And, staring him in the face, the wedding ring that waited to be placed on Eunice's slender finger. It was a simple, flat-profile band of the purest platinum, with rounded sides that perfectly matched the engagement ring Eunice had accepted from him just months ago.

He took up the pen and began to scribble a letter.

Dear Eunice,

I trust this letter finds you well and that you are still having a nice time with the Farquhars. Do give them my best regards.

Things have been pretty hectic here.

You see, contrary to what was expected, I have been out on a couple of sorties with the French squadron I'm attached to. They were hell, Eunice. I've nothing but admiration for these bomber crews.

A bit of bad news. Butch Paderewski has died. Staś is pretty cut up about it. Me too, to be honest.

Eunice, I have been thinking. It was inconsiderate and, frankly, damned irresponsible of me to ask you to marry me. I don't know what I was thinking. There's a war on, and any of us could be killed in an instant. I'd hate to think of you left like poor Milly, a single mother with the child of a dead airman.

You have probably worked out what I am about to write. I'm calling it off, Eunice darling.

I want to thank you for the happy times, and even for some of the difficult times we have had together. I'll never forget you.

Please don't look at this as a rejection. Think of it more as a release.

Yours ever, Gus

Gus read the letter through. *Bloody nonsense*, he thought, scrunching it up and throwing it into the paper basket. He took another sip of the Scotch. Then he selected a clean sheet of paper and began again, amending the final paragraph:

Eunice, I have been thinking. I made a mistake when I proposed to you. I'm not the man for you. I'm calling it off. I want to thank you for the happy times, and even for some of the difficult times we have had together.
Yours sincerely,
Gus

He read this letter, tore it in half and threw the pieces into the basket. He topped up his drink then sat down to start again.

Dear Eunice,
I trust this letter finds you well.
There is no easy way of writing this. I have found another lover. Our engagement is over.
Yours sincerely,
Gus

Once again, he read the letter through. God, it was terse, he thought. But it would have to do. He folded the paper and pushed it into an envelope he'd previously addressed and stamped. *That's it*, he thought. *Finished.*

The next thing to do was talk to Izzy. Theirs was another unhealthy, perhaps eventually damaging relationship. Gus knew he needed to end it. He was overwhelmed by a deep, dark feeling of emptiness. He had to move on.

He'd never felt like this before. It was as though a dense curtain had descended over him, body and soul. It seemed to blot the light from his vision; he felt the heavy weight of it across his shoulders.

He invited Izzy out for a walk around the city walls of York, walls that had been built hundreds of years before by the Romans. Walls that, could they talk, might have related the many conversations of enticement, romance, rejection and, no doubt, separation they had borne silent witness to.

"Look Izzy," he said, "there's no easy way of saying this, but I just can't handle our relationship."

She stopped and turned to face him. As she did so, Gus saw tears were already welling up in her pale grey eyes.

"Please don't misunderstand me. It isn't that I don't want it. You. It's just… I can't explain…"

"You don't need to. I knew it couldn't last between you and me. I always said that we're from totally different backgrounds."

"It isn't that. Believe me."

"What is it then? Me?"

"No. It's this bloody war. The war brought us together, gave us the chance. But it's messed me up so much, Izzy. I just don't know who I am or what I need any longer."

Izzy looked at Gus, waiting for him to explain.

"We could carry on just being friends, perhaps?" he suggested.

"I don't think so, Gus. I think a clean break might be better."

"All or nothing?"

"You see, I think I'd always be hoping you might change your mind."

"I won't," he said.

"Then it's goodbye, Gus." As she turned away and began to walk off in the opposite direction, Gus thought he heard her sobs.

Following the conversation with Izzy, Gus retreated to his room. He stood by the window and looked out at the damp Yorkshire afternoon. Then, overcome by the dreadful sadness of the situation, he dropped onto the bed and silently wept.

The next morning Flight Lieutenant Colson of the Royal Air Force Police Special Investigation Branch arrived at Elvington to interview Gus. When Gus got the news of his visit, he felt decidedly uncomfortable. He'd put one mess behind him, and now another had resurfaced. When would it end?

Once again, they were going to use Jimmy's office. Gus hurried from the mess. *Better get this over and done with*, he thought. When he got there, the adjutant wasn't present, just a corporal who waved Gus through to the office. *Jimmy's avoiding me*, thought Gus.

"Good morning, Beaumont," said Colson. "Sit down."

Gus replied with a nod. There it was again. That bloody twitch. He wondered if Colson could see it. Would he think it was a sign of guilt?

"What can I do for you? More questions?"

"No. It's what I can do for you, old boy. I just wanted to let you know that you are no longer under investigation."

Gus took a deep breath. It felt as if a weight had suddenly been lifted from him. "That's a relief. Thanks for letting me know."

"You're welcome."

"Pursuing other leads, are you?"

"The case is closed. Well, not closed, exactly," said Colson. "On ice, you might say. We've investigated all leads and have come to the conclusion that Squadron Leader Grindlethorpe was unlucky. He was killed by a random petty thief. The motive was robbery, simple as that. But there are no fingerprints, no witnesses and no murder weapon, so we have nothing to go on. If and when there are more leads, we can look again. That's why I say on ice."

"I see," said Gus. "Well, as I say, it is a relief. Did you come all the way up here to tell me that?"

"No," said Colson. "I need you to sign a statement. Just for the record, you know. Bloody bureaucracy, if you ask me, but it's the way of the world these days. I've got something typed. It's based on what you told Detective Inspector Ruskin; I've been to see him in London. Do read it through first, by all means."

Gus took the sheets of paper and scanned through them. It was, as Colson suggested, an account based on what he had said previously, though it was short and several details were missing. He signed it and passed the papers back.

"Well, I must be off," said Colson. "Work to do and all that. There is a war on, after all." He stood, saluted and left.

The account Gus had signed detailed his whereabouts and movements at the time of Grindlethorpe's death. It also contained the statement of his innocence. But it did not mention Grindlethorpe's diary and suspicions, or the wallet full of money that had been found on the squadron leader's body. *Grindlethorpe couldn't possibly have been killed by a thief*, thought Gus.

CHAPTER 20

A few days later, Gus received a call from Wing Commander Sir Alexander Peacock, asking him to drop by the SOE offices. Tired, demoralised and depressed, Gus boarded the train to London. When he'd shaved that morning, he'd caught a glimpse of his face in the mirror and hadn't recognised himself. His skin was grey and there were bags as dark as bruises under both eyes. Now, sitting in a carriage full of people, he wondered what they thought of him.

When he arrived in the capital, he noticed London was a degree or two warmer than Elvington, but equally as wet. From King's Cross, Gus walked to Baker Street and the SOE offices. He got to Peacock's office at eleven-thirty.

"Good morning, Gustaw," said Peacock. "I understand you have been interviewed by the police. Wanted to talk to you about it. Oh, do have a seat. Tea?"

"Yes please, sir," said Gus, sitting down.

"Well, what do we make of it, Gustaw?"

"How much do you know?"

"Very little. That's why you're here."

"The civilian police were about to arrest me for Grindlethorpe's murder."

"Were they, by George?"

"Then the RAF Police intervened. A Flight Lieutenant Colson took over the case. Now they've put it on ice."

"On ice? Why have they've done that?"

"I don't know, sir. Colson thinks Grindlethorpe was a random victim. He thinks the killer was a thief."

"And what do you think?"

"I don't believe Colson."

"What, exactly, don't you believe?"

"That Grindlethorpe was killed by a random thief."

"Why not?"

"Because of what Detective Inspector Ruskin from Scotland Yard told me. He let it slip that the police found Grindlethorpe's wallet on his body. I think Ruskin said it contained five pounds and there were some coins in his pocket. A thief would have taken the lot. Ruskin thinks there was another motive."

"Does he, by Jove? And what makes him think that?"

"Grindlethorpe kept a diary. He thought somebody was tailing him, perhaps intending to kill him. Ruskin thought it might be me."

"Was it you?"

"Of course not."

"But Grindlethorpe mentioned you, did he?"

"Yes."

"Who else did he mention? Who did he think might want to bump him off?"

"I'm not sure. But Ruskin quizzed me about Krawiec and wanted to know about the French Resistance cell we brought back from Dieppe. So Grindlethorpe may have suspected any of them, I suppose."

"Well, if Titus suspected Krawiec, you and the French, I'll bet he suspected me, too."

Gus frowned. "Why on earth would Grindlethorpe think you would want to kill him, Sir Alex?"

"It sounds to me as if he was paranoid. It's a good job I have an alibi. I was sick on the day he was killed, as you know. My daily, Mrs Samworth, was so worried about me that she stayed the night. She brought her daughter with her and they both used the spare room. One or the other came in every hour to make sure I was still in the land of the living."

"I'm sorry to hear that, sir. Were you really so bad?"

"Probably not. But Mrs Samworth, well, she's a bit of a fusspot. She made me inhale some horrible-smelling stuff. Friars' Balsam, she called it. It loosened things up, though, I must say."

"Well, that certainly sounds like a solid alibi to me, sir."

"And then the Royal Air Force Police intervened, you say. What do you think of that?"

"No idea, sir. But Colson told me if there are any more leads, he'd look into the case again. But I think that's a load of rubbish."

"Why?"

"Because then it will be a civilian investigation, won't it? The RAF Police won't be involved."

"Yes. Yes, you're quite right. And it's most irregular, actually, that the snowdrops are involved at all. You see, it is entirely a civil matter. A murder took place in London and Scotland Yard is the proper force to investigate it."

"That's what Ruskin told Colson. But Colson had a letter. He told Ruskin it was no longer his case."

"This letter, Gustaw — any idea who signed it off?"

"Colson told Ruskin it was an order making it clear the investigation was a military matter. He said it was signed by high authority at both the Home Office and the Air Chief Marshal's office."

"And now Flight Lieutenant Colson tells you you're no longer under investigation because the murderer is a common thief, which we know is a load of bunkum because Titus had his wallet full of money still on him when the body was found."

"Exactly," said Gus.

The wing commander remained silent for a few moments.

"Somebody at the Air Chief Marshal's office is trying to hide something. Maybe the Home Office too, though I doubt it. But do you know what, Gustaw?"

"What, Sir Alex?"

"We're never going to find out, because it has absolutely nothing to do with us," said Peacock.

Gus was stunned. It wasn't like Peacock to be interested in a subject and then let it drop like that.

"The RAF Police are no longer interested in you, Gustaw. You're not a suspect. Nor am I, for that matter, and so that's it. Understand me?"

"Yes, of course, Sir Alex." *Why is he being so forceful?* thought Gus.

"Now, about our French guests up at Elvington. I want to know how they're getting on. But first, how about a spot of lunch? Care to join me, Gustaw?"

"Yes, thank you. That would be nice."

"There's a place around the corner that does very good fried haddock and chips. My treat."

Over lunch, Gus briefed the wing commander on the French squadron. Then he let the older man chat away, only half listening. His ears pricked up when Peacock said, "By the way, I'll arrange for you to leave RAF Elvington and get back to Tempsford and 161 Squadron, if you like?"

"Yes. Yes, please," said Gus, relieved. "That would make life much easier. Thank you, sir."

Gus left Peacock at the café soon after lunch. He walked slowly north along Baker Street towards Euston, watching the circulation of cars, lorries and red London buses as he walked along. The rhythm of the traffic was untroubled, which somehow reminded him of peacetime.

As he watched a blue Austin drive away down Euston Road towards King's Cross, he became aware that something wrong. There were far too many questions. Why had the Grindlethorpe investigation been taken away from Scotland Yard when it should have been a civilian matter? Why had Peacock brought himself under suspicion? And why had the usually inquisitive wing commander warned Gus off following anything up?

Gus wondered what was written in that diary.

On impulse, he turned and made a beeline for a public telephone box. He dialled the number for Scotland Yard.

"Scotland Yard, who do you want me to put you through to, please?"

"I want to speak to Detective Inspector Ruskin. Tell him it's Flight Lieutenant Beaumont, would you?"

Ruskin was on the line almost immediately. "Flight Lieutenant Beaumont. Nice of you to call. What can I do for you?"

"I need to talk to you. I'm here in London — can you meet me somewhere?"

There was a pause. Gus heard coughing in the background. Eventually, the detective came back to him. "Yes, I think I can re-jig things to see you."

"Shall I come over to you?" asked Gus.

"No. It will have to be somewhere else."

"Do you know the Royal Geographical Society buildings? Lowther Lodge?"

"Of course I know. I'm a policeman," laughed Ruskin, but his laughter quickly turned to coughing, which he found difficult to stop. "Sorry. Yes, I know the place. On the south side of Hyde Park, isn't it?"

"Would half past three be all right?" asked Gus.

"Yes."

"See you there," said Gus and hung up.

CHAPTER 21

When Ruskin arrived at Lowther Lodge, Gus was at reception to meet him. They took a table in one of the smaller meeting rooms.

"I didn't realise you were a Fellow here, Flight Lieutenant."

"I'm not, I'm just a member. My father was a Fellow. In 1924 he took part in the third British expedition to climb Mount Everest."

"Did he indeed? What a thing. I used to enjoy a bit of mountaineering myself. Oh, don't look so surprised. I haven't always been this age, you know. Or this girth." He laughed. "No, I used to be quite a fit young man back in my day. I hiked in Yorkshire, Wales, Scotland. I loved those mountains." He paused. "Now then, Flight Lieutenant, what's all this about?"

"I say, could we drop the formalities, do you think? I'm Gus, or Bouncer to my friends. You are?"

"Sam, but the lads call me Governor. Or just Guv. I'm easy with that. But you know I've been taken off the case," Ruskin replied, pulling a packet of cigarettes from his pocket.

"Bit irregular, that, isn't it? You being taken off the Grindlethorpe case?"

"Damned irregular, yes. I've put in a complaint, but it's getting nowhere."

"Do you know that the RAF Police have put the case on the backburner? They say it's a random killing done for financial gain. Robbery."

"That's simply impossible."

"Yes. You told me about Grindlethorpe's wallet, and the diary. So, Guv, you believe he was being followed by someone and sized up to be murdered?"

"Slow down, young man. I don't necessarily think that. But I believe *he* thought he was."

"And I was on his list of suspects?"

"Yes."

"And you think I did it."

"You're going too quick again, Gus. Slow down."

"But you were about to arrest me, just before Colson stepped in."

"That didn't mean I thought it was you that did it. I needed to carry on the interview with you under caution. It was a formality. Look, Squadron Leader Grindlethorpe died between ten o'clock on Thursday evening and four on Friday morning. You previously told me you were alone during that time and spent most of it in your fiancée's flat in Hampstead?"

"That's correct. No one to back me up, I'm afraid," said Gus.

"Well, I'm sorry to be so blunt, but you disliked Grindlethorpe, had threatened to kill him, and don't have an alibi for that night. You were, in fact, a chief suspect, until…"

"Until Colson stepped in."

"But that doesn't mean I think you did it. I have an instinct. I've done this job for more years than I'd like to think, and I've developed a nose for criminals. In my opinion, you're not one."

"Thanks. But on paper I'm a suspect. I and I alone know that I'm innocent of Grindlethorpe's murder."

The policeman nodded and smoked, saying nothing.

"It wasn't me, Guv. And, frankly, I'd like to prove it wasn't me. Remind me, who else was on Grindlethorpe's list?"

"Wing Commander Peacock."

"In bed with the flu. Carers popping in to check on him every hour. Two of them."

"Chap called Krawiec. Some French Resistance fighters. Eunice Hesketh…"

"Eunice? Bloody hell."

"She's your fiancée?"

"Was," said Gus.

"Was? Oh dear, I'm sorry."

"Long story, but why on earth would Grindlethorpe suspect Eunice? Anyway, she at least does have an alibi. Eunice was up in Scotland on the night in question. I saw her off on a train from King's Cross that had a first scheduled stop at Doncaster."

"There's also Duncan Farquhar, but he's unlikely, as Grindlethorpe suggested he's a POW. Is that correct?"

"It is, he is a prisoner of the Germans. Captured at Dieppe."

"So, Peacock, Eunice and Duncan have alibis. That leaves you, Krawiec and the French Resistance chaps. If I exclude you, it leaves just Krawiec and the French."

"Then you need to interview them, Guv."

"Sorry. I'm off the case."

"Officially, you're off the case. But unofficially?"

"More than my job's worth. I can't go around interviewing suspects willy-nilly."

"Perhaps not, but I can. Under your direction."

The tea had arrived. Ruskin was deep in thought, considering the situation as Gus poured tea.

"Right," said Ruskin, clearly having made a decision, "what can you tell me about Krawiec and Operation… What was it called?"

"Lodz," said Gus, "Operation Lodz." He took a sip of tea and a deep breath. Ruskin had taken out his notebook and a pencil. Where to begin? "Look, Guv. Lodz, and Krawiec's work, are covered by the Official Secrets Act. I can't say too much."

"Just the salient bits."

"Squadron Leader Piotr Krawiec is a Pole. He sometimes goes by the Anglicised version of his name, Peter Taylor. He was a Russian Air Force officer in the Great War. After the war, he went into the Polish civil service. Foreign department. I met him before the war, with Sir Alex, as a matter of fact. He was at the Polish embassy here in London. Now RAF, obviously. All the Poles are. Krawiec is a leading light in a secret Polish unit. He's based in Essex. I know where, but it's better I don't say."

"I see. And I suppose that's where Operation Lodz comes in, yes?"

"Yes. Lodz was a hush-hush mission to land agents and equipment into occupied Poland. It was the first operation to have an all-Polish crew. Well, all-polish speakers. Krawiec argued they would be more familiar with the country. If they were downed, they'd have a much better chance of getting away. I was navigator on the Halifax that dropped the agents in."

Ruskin raised an eyebrow. "I see. Do carry on."

"Krawiec met Sir Alex and Grindlethorpe. He had intelligence that the Soviet government was dropping supplies for the Armia Ludowa…"

"And that is…?"

"The Polish People's Army. Krawiec said that the Armia Ludowa has never shown any loyalty to the Polish Government-in-Exile or the Polish Home Army. They're communists. Krawiec thinks they're cosying up to Uncle Joe in Moscow. The Soviets were aiding them because Stalin wants to see a communist Poland after the war."

"This is all very political."

"It's all political, Guv. Krawiec argued that Britian and the exiled Poles should support the NSZ — that's a nasty, extreme right-wing Polish resistance group. He said it was the third largest underground armed force fighting in Poland. The NSZ hate the Reds. Krawiec insisted it would fight the communists wherever it encountered them."

"So, Lodz was all about politics? Who we support, who we don't?"

"That's correct. Post-war politics. The NSZ is almost as bad as the Nazis. But Krawiec wanted to support it. He argued that as the SOE already drops supplies, weapons, ammunition, explosives, it was only a small step to drop agents. He had a small team ready at Audley End. He wanted to drop them in so they could link up with the NSZ — organise them to fight the Reds and eliminate the Polish People's Army. Krawiec said it was simple. The exiled Poles couldn't let a communist Poland happen after the war and the British Government should support them in that."

"What did the others think?"

"Peacock and Grindlethorpe agreed, and I suppose the strategy of supporting the right against the left in Poland must have had sign-off higher up. So Operation Lodz went ahead."

"And it was successful?"

"No. Sadly, there were machine gunners waiting for the agents at the drop zone. From the Halifax we saw fire flashes from the ground on all sides of the DZ. Small arms. The agents were being shot at."

"So, they'd been rumbled? The Germans knew they were coming?"

"The Poles thought they'd been betrayed," said Gus.

"But you don't?"

"We don't know," replied Gus. "There was an inquest into Lodz, led by Sir Alex. Krawiec was there. I was called in to give evidence. I told them exactly what happened."

"Tell me."

"The Halifax approached the DZ at two hundred and fifty feet. The pilot was called Błaszczykowski — nice chap. He was flying as slowly as he dared, about sixty-five knots. I went to the back to wish the men good luck, but almost as soon as I got there the red light came on. When it changed to green, the dispatcher sent them all down the Joe hole and I watched the chutes open. Then the pilot turned for a second run and the same dispatcher chucked out the supplies. I went back to the cockpit. Before I got there, the dispatcher was shouting that small arms fire had opened up. There was nothing we could do. Błaszczykowski turned to port so we could try to see what was going on. All I saw was shots coming towards the parachutes from the ground surrounding the DZ. There was no returning fire.

"Krawiec was outraged. He shouted that they didn't stand a chance. They'd been butchered. Killed in their parachutes. He was right about that. But he went further. He maintained that Operation Lodz had been betrayed. He said he'd kill whoever had betrayed his men."

"Did he suspect anyone?"

"Yes. He thought it was Squadron Leader Grindlethorpe."

Ruskin continued making notes. "Go on."

"Sir Alex asked who knew the location of the drop zone."

"And who did?"

"Three of us in the UK. Squadron Leader Krawiec, Squadron Leader Grindlethorpe and myself. And the NSZ on the ground in Poland, of course."

"What about the pilot? Błaszczykowski?"

"No. I told him the route to fly only once we were airborne. He didn't have a clue beforehand."

"How many of the partisans on the ground knew about the DZ?"

"Hard to estimate. Krawiec maintained he'd only informed the cell leader. That would be usual. But we just don't know how many others knew the details before the night."

"And what did the NSZ people think happened?"

"They were sure somebody here in London tipped off the Germans. They lost seven of their own people on the ground, alongside the agents."

"Who on earth in London would tip off the Germans?" asked Ruskin. "Krawiec thought it was Grindlethorpe, but why? What motive would Grindlethorpe have for betraying Operation Lodz?"

"There is a possibility," muttered Gus.

"Go on."

"The Polish agents dropped into Poland during Lodz were all Jews — recruited from Palestine, actually. As I told you in Elvington, Grindlethorpe had been a supporter of Oswald Mosley."

"How do you know that?"

"Sir Alex said he'd been looking into Grindlethorpe's history. Grindlethorpe was an anti-Semite. That's one reason he had it in for me. I've told you all this."

"Gus, tell me, do you think Squadron Leader Grindlethorpe betrayed Operation Lodz?"

"No. No, I don't. Though nothing's impossible. I think Krawiec was wrong. Nobody in London tipped off the Germans or the Armia Ludowa. It was one of their own. Perhaps one of them was captured and tortured, though that's unlikely. They'd have called off Lodz if they thought they'd been exposed. But somebody on the ground in Poland may have tipped off the Germans deliberately, perhaps for money, or maybe they were simply lax. Or it was just bad luck. But I don't believe for one minute that a tip-off came from this end, from London. As much as I disliked him, I find it impossible to believe Squadron Leader Grindlethorpe was a traitor."

"Thank you."

"But it doesn't matter what I think, does it?" said Gus.

"What do you mean?"

"I mean Krawiec said in public that he'd kill the person who betrayed Operation Lodz, and he was convinced that person was Grindlethorpe."

"Yes, he did. We need to know what Krawiec was doing on the night of Grindlethorpe's murder," said Ruskin. "The problem is, I can't very well go up to Essex and ask him."

"You may not be able to, Guv, but I can," said Gus.

CHAPTER 22

Detective Inspector Ruskin finished his tea. "We've been here too long," he said. "People here may know me. We'll have to make a move. You see me to reception and bid me a fond farewell. Leave ten minutes after. Outside, turn right and walk down the road until you get to South Kensington tube station. I'll meet you there, just outside."

They rose and walked to reception together. Ruskin got his hat and coat, then Gus waved him off into the rain. He then mused over a couple of pamphlets for ten minutes or so and left the Royal Geographical Society as instructed.

Ten minutes later, he saw DI Ruskin waiting outside South Kensington tube station as promised.

"Fancy a pint?" asked Ruskin. "My treat."

"Yes please," said Gus.

They rushed across the road, dodging traffic and side-stepping the puddles that were already forming. They ducked into a large pub opposite the tube station. Ruskin took off his hat, pushing his way through the crowded saloon and towards the busy bar. He bought them beers and brought them to a small table in the corner which Gus had found. The two men sat down.

"Now," said Ruskin, taking a long draught of his pint, "let's have a chat about this French Resistance business, shall we?"

"It's all connected with Operation Jubilee," said Gus, "the Combined Operations raid on Dieppe this summer. I was crewing a Lockheed Hudson landing a small group of Joes…"

"Joes?"

"Sorry — let's just call them specials."

"Specials? You're talking about secret agents?"

Gus nodded. "I was transporting a small group of specials into Normandy. Their job was to link up with a Resistance cell near Dieppe. Some of the names are already in the open, so there's no harm telling you. There were three of them: Duncan Farquhar, Eunice Hesketh and a wireless operator. I didn't know him at all."

"Tell me," interrupted Ruskin, "are RAF pilots and crews on that sort of job supposed to know the agents they are landing and picking up?"

"It isn't usual, shall we say. Anyway, a bit like in the Lodz operation, the Germans were waiting for us. They had heavy machine guns positioned by the landing zone. They hit the plane before we landed. We lost the pilot, but everyone else was uninjured. We found out that one of the cell had been taken in for questioning and assumed that was how the Jerries knew where the landing zone would be. But no, it turned out this chap had been pulled in by the French gendarmes, and he was later released…"

"So how did the Germans know where you were going to land?"

"Exactly! How on earth did they know? Later, other members of the cell were taken in — this time by the Gestapo, so somehow the cell had been blown. But that's not all. The cell had put together a detailed report on the German defences and positions all around Dieppe. They sent a copy to England with an RAF pilot in a Lysander. The report never got to Peacock."

"Maybe the plane was shot down."

"I'd be sure to know. It's my squadron."

"So how do you explain it?"

"There's only one possibility. The Lysander landed safely and the report was handed over. Then someone intercepted it. Somebody was deliberately concealing information from Peacock and his office. And there is only one person who might have met that Lysander."

"Who?" asked Ruskin.

"Squadron Leader Titus Grindlethorpe. He was part of the briefing team and often in on the debrief. Those Lysander flights always came into RAF Tangmere. Grindlethorpe would be there to meet and debrief the pilot. Part of his job."

"Why would Grindlethorpe do such a thing?"

"I don't know, but I do have a theory."

"Tell me."

"The cell was communist. We know Grindlethorpe hated Reds." Gus frowned. "Wait a minute, there's something else. Peacock thought Grindlethorpe was living a bit beyond his means. You know, he lived in an expensive part of town; he couldn't possibly afford Regent's Park on a squadron leader's pay. I remember Peacock being curious about where Grindlethorpe's money was coming from."

"He thought Grindlethorpe could be taking dirty money from someone?"

"It's possible. Do you still have Grindlethorpe's diary?"

"I'm not sure. We had it, of course. But Colson may have confiscated it. I can check back at the office. Why do you ask?"

"Grindlethorpe might have written about the Dieppe report. If you find the diary, you could check for entries around, let's say, the middle of July to mid-September. That'll cover Jubilee and it might throw up something."

"Yes. I can do that. If we can find the diary, of course. Mind you, it's of academic interest only."

"What do you mean?"

"If Wing Commander Peacock had questions about where Grindlethorpe's money was coming from and he even had a whiff of suspicion that Grindlethorpe had concealed the report, well, that in itself could provide motive enough."

"Agreed, but Peacock has an alibi. He was ill. He told me he has witnesses that can say he was in bed with the flu most of that day and all of that night."

For a while Ruskin said nothing; he just stared at his empty pint glass. Then, in that gravelly voice of his, he said, "And he told you all this? Volunteered the information?"

"Yes."

"A bit odd, isn't it?"

It was, now that Gus thought about it. Peacock wasn't a suspect as far as Gus knew, so why was he so keen to let Gus know he had an alibi?

"Shall we have another?" asked Ruskin.

"Good idea. I'll get them."

When Gus returned with the drinks, Ruskin had more questions for him.

"Tell me about this French cell. What happened to them?"

"There were four of them, originally. The old man, the one who'd been questioned by the police, he was re-arrested. Soon afterwards, another — a woman — was picked up. Those two would have been tortured then killed by the Gestapo. The other two came back with the Dieppe commandos. Men, both of them. Baudouin and Claude. Covers, I expect, not their real names."

"We need to talk to them. I wonder how we might track them down? Do you think Peacock will know?"

"If he doesn't know, he can find out."

"Peacock seems to have his finger in every pie, doesn't he? We need a plan. This is what we'll do: first, you need to talk to this chap Krawiec. I want you to go to Essex and speak to him. Find out what he was doing on the night Grindlethorpe was murdered."

"I can't just ask him if he killed Grindlethorpe."

"Of course not. Approach it in a more roundabout way. Krawiec will be aware of Grindlethorpe's death, but he doesn't know he's a suspect. He won't expect you to be investigating it. So don't go barging in, no. You could let him know that you were under suspicion but the RAF Police have closed the case. Say you want to clear your name and that's why you're interested. See what he says."

"All right, that might work."

"Second, we need to find the two Frenchmen — Baudouin and Claude."

"Like I said, Peacock will know how to contact them, but he's warned me off asking about the case, remember?"

"Better not to involve him."

"I'll have to think about it, then. Leave it with me."

"Once we've tracked them down, we need to find out more about them and what they've been up to. You'll need to talk to both of them, preferably not together."

"Wait a minute," said Gus. "Eunice may know where they are. She brought them back to the UK and handed them over. They were going to be invited to our wedding, but... Yes, there's a pretty good chance Eunice will know."

"Excellent," said Ruskin, finishing his pint. "When will you make a start?"

"I need to be back in RAF Tempsford tonight. Peacock's having me transferred back to the squadron. That will take a week or so, I expect. All being well, I'll go up to Edinburgh the day after tomorrow and see Eunice there."

"That's my boy. I'll make a detective of you yet," said Ruskin, taking the packet of cigarettes from his pocket. He took a long drag and started coughing, and before long was bent double on the chair.

Eventually the coughing fit subsided. "Sorry," said Ruskin, "I really must kick the habit."

CHAPTER 23

With much going through his mind, Gus took a train which made its way slowly through north London, bound for the Midlands. He'd made a promise to Ruskin that he would speak to Eunice and then visit Krawiec, and he would. But these things could wait. Gus was spending the night at his former squadron at Tempsford, where he could relax with his friends in the mess and break the news of his impending return to them.

He took a train to Sandy and got off at the station there. Because he wasn't expected, there was no transport to meet him, but Gus managed to hitch a lift in a lorry crammed with a Home Guard troop that was heading to St Neots.

Gus jumped down from the lorry at the gates to RAF Tempsford.

"Thanks very much!" he shouted to the elder men and young lads.

"You're most welcome, sir," came the reply, "and give Jerry one from us when you see him next, won't you?"

"I certainly will!" Gus promised as he made his way to the gate and showed his pass to the soldier on guard. Luckily, it was one he recognised.

"Nice to see you back, sir," said the squaddie, saluting.

Gus returned the salute as he strolled through the gates and made his way over to a low building ahead of him. Once in the mess, he was greeted heartily by the officers of 161 Squadron.

"Great to have you back with us, Bouncer," said Doggie Russell, blowing pipe tobacco at Gus. "You must have lots to tell us. Can I get you a drink?"

"I'll say, Doggie, and I promise to reveal all in the mess later, but I really need a wash first. Can you point me towards my billet?"

"Same room as before — we saved it for you. Now, you go unpack and make yourself comfy."

"Oh, I don't have much kit, as you can see. Any chance I could borrow a clean shirt from one of you?"

"Sure, have one of mine," said Flying Officer Thomas 'Lippy' Granger. "You're the same size as me. I'll bring one up."

"Thanks, Lippy."

The bath was hot and made Gus feel drowsy. He wallowed for a while until the water grew tepid. After the luxury of his bath, he shaved, dressed and made his way to the mess dining room.

It was busy. Gus spotted Doggie standing by the bar. He walked over to his friend.

"What will you have, Bouncer?"

"Beer please, Doggie. I'm parched."

"One for you, Arthur?" Doggie asked a young-looking pilot officer, new to Gus.

"I'll have a beer, too. Thanks."

Doggie turned to Gus. "So, what exactly *have* you been up to?"

Gus explained about the French squadron, and mentioned Butch's death and his split with Eunice, but was careful not to let slip anything about the murder investigation. Nor did he mention Izzy Parry.

"Well, you're home now, my old china, and you can relax."

"Thanks, Doggie. And the best news is, I'm to be posted back here!"

"That's fantastic news," said Doggie. "Let's have another drink."

"Listen up, boys!" shouted Arthur. "Bouncer's coming back to us. Drinks all round. On him."

Gus ate with the others and, for a while at least, forgot his worries.

After their meal, Arthur Bacon, the young pilot officer who'd cost Gus a round of drinks and who happened to be a gifted pianist, went over to the upright piano. He opened the cover, sat down and began to play. He was soon joined by Lippy Granger on the trumpet, and the pair played some popular tunes — first a few ragtime numbers and then the more contemporary swing. Shortly, the mess was calling out for Doggie to sing for them.

"Come on, Doggie, give us a song," insisted Gus.

"All right, if I must," he said, placing his pipe beside an ashtray.

Gus soon regretted his encouragement of his friends, however. Arthur and Lippy began playing Glenn Miller's 'Moonlight Serenade'. As they played, Gus recalled dancing a slow Foxtrot to this very tune with Eunice. He was even more regretful when Doggie began singing Mitchell Parish's words to the ballad. As the duo played and Doggie crooned, Gus became maudlin.

Then Doggie stopped singing to address the mess. "Actually," he announced, "I've been working on a 161 Squadron version of this, and I dedicate it to our very own Flight Lieutenant Bouncer Beaumont."

The piano sounded an introduction, Lippy's trumpet joined in and then Doggie's rich, baritone voice rang out through the mess:

"I fly through the sky

And the wish that I have is for moonlight.
I stare for a flare,
Flaming glare, to guide me down safely.
The lights, they are shining
Bright light serenade."

The sounds of laughter and clapping echoed through the mess, but Doggie hadn't finished.

"As I wait for those Joes
My one wish — only wish — is for no light.
Just dark. Solid dark,
For any light will give the Boche targets
To shoot at. To shoot a
Bright light fusillade.
We take off. Going home
And the wish that I have is for moonlight
I look for a route
But am lost and can't seem to find my way.
My compass is broken.
Moonlight serenade."

As Doggie and the others finished, the officers showed their appreciation with riotous applause, banging on tables and cheering.

"Three cheers for Doggie! Hip, hip…"

"Hurrah!"

"And three loud cheers for the lost cause, Bouncer! Hip, hip…"

"Hurrah!"

Two days later, Gus made the journey to Edinburgh. He considered taking a taxi directly from Waverley station to the home of Duncan's parents, but that would have got him there too quickly. He wasn't ready to barge in on Eunice. Instead, he took a stroll around the new town, then slogged his way up the hill to the Old Town. He walked along the Royal Mile between Holyrood Palace and the castle. He'd tried phoning Eunice three times the previous day, but she was never there to speak to him. At least, that was what the Farquhars maintained.

Frankly, he was dreading meeting her again. The prospect was more terrifying than crossing the Channel in a Lysander. Almost as bad as going up in a bloody Short Stirling.

Mr and Mrs Farquhar lived in Stockbridge and Gus found a cab by the castle. The driver took him once again over ground he'd already covered, through the New Town and north. He stopped close to an old house by the small bridge which spanned the Water of Leith.

"It's that one, there, sir. Blue door."

"Thanks. How much do I owe you?"

"That'll be two and fourpence, if you please, sir."

Gus paid the taxi driver with a half crown coin, telling him to keep the change, and climbed the few steps leading up to the Farquhars' front door. He rang the bell and waited.

Eventually, an elderly man opened the door and considered Gus. "Can I help you?"

"Mr Farquhar? My name is Gus Beaumont and I'm a friend of your son, Duncan. However, it's Miss Hesketh I've come to see. On business. Is she in, by any chance?"

"Aye, she's here," said Mr Farquhar, offering a hand, which Gus shook. "Won't you come in? I'll give young Eunice a shout."

Gus crossed the threshold and removed his cap in the Farquhars' entrance hall.

"Eunice!" Mr Farquhar called up the stairs. "There's a young man here to see you. An air force officer." He turned to Gus. "Did you say you're a friend of Duncan's?"

"That's correct. It was so unlucky for him, to be captured again."

"Aye. Unlucky."

"I was there when he was captured, as it happens."

"You were? Well, perhaps you could tell me a little…" The old man stopped talking as Eunice appeared on the landing and began to descend the stairs.

Gus gazed up at her. She didn't quite look herself, he thought. More withdrawn.

"Hello, Eunice," he said, nervously.

"Gus," she replied with a nod. There was no smile on her face, and he noticed that she didn't meet his gaze. Why should she? He'd treated her appallingly.

"A bit of a problem has cropped up." He turned to Mr Farquhar. "I'm sorry, sir, but please could we have a chat in private? National security, I'm sure you'll understand."

"Aye. You two go and sit yourselves in there." He pointed to the room to the right of the stairwell. "I'll make a pot of tea. It'll take me a good fifteen minutes, I'm sure, and don't you worry, I'll knock before I come in with it."

"Thank you, sir."

Eunice led the way into what turned out to be a sitting room decorated with Victoriana.

"What's all this about?" she asked, icily.

Gus looked at his ex-fiancée. "I'm a suspect in a murder investigation, Eunice. The Metropolitan Police think I killed Titus Grindlethorpe."

"What? I don't believe it. Why on earth would anyone suspect you of murder, Gus? Anyway, how does it involve me?"

"Frankly, we need your help."

"We?"

Gus told Eunice everything he knew about the murder and subsequent investigation. "I need to clear my name, you see, even though the snowdrops have put the case on ice."

"I must say, it's all very intriguing. It's just like the Agatha Christie I'm reading."

"What, *The Sittaford Mystery*? Are you still on that?"

"Oh gosh, no. I finished that ages ago and have read another four or five since. I'm reading *The Secret of Chimneys* at the moment. It's about this young man, Anthony Cade, who discovers more than he bargained for when he agrees to deliver a parcel to an English country house. Christie's so very good. She lays out all the evidence and, if I'm thorough, I find I can usually spot the killer before I get to the end of the book."

"We'll make a sleuth of you yet, Eunice," said Gus with a smile.

"You said Grindlethorpe even suspected that I wanted to kill him?"

"He seems to have suspected just about every one of us."

"Me, though? I mean…"

"I think the poor man was paranoid."

"Well, that's a new one. I never thought I'd hear you being sympathetic towards Titus Grindlethorpe."

"I'm not sympathetic, but I do need to clear my name. Even though the RAF Police have called off the investigation, eventually it will go against me, I know. I need your help, Eunice."

She looked at him intently.

"Eunice, I … I'm…"

"Stop! Don't say a thing, Gus. Not about us. Not a single word."

The look on Eunice's face told him she was in no mood to discuss anything apart from business.

"All right," he said meekly.

"What do you think I can do to help?"

"Find the whereabouts of Baudouin and Claude and let Detective Inspector Ruskin and I know." He looked at her. "I wouldn't ask, but..."

"I don't know why I should help you out, after ... but I'll do it. Give me a day or so to tidy things up here, then I'll come down to London."

"That's awfully good of you, Eunice..."

There was a knock at the door.

"Come in," called Eunice.

It was Duncan's parents. Mrs Farquhar carried a tray with a teapot and four cups on it. Her husband was holding a packet of biscuits.

"So, you're a friend of our Duncan's," said the old woman.

"Yes. Miss Hesketh and I are finished now — why not sit down with us? I'll tell you all about what happened during the Dieppe raid — with Duncan, I mean."

"Yes," said Mrs Farquhar, "that would be nice."

Within the parameters of what he could divulge and what was safe to tell them, Gus explained what had happened. How he, Gus, had survived a crashlanding and was stranded in Normandy, how Duncan had been injured with a badly broken leg, and how even Lord Lovat's commandos couldn't carry him down to the beaches where boats were ready to take them. Duncan had been left behind and captured, and was now incarcerated in a German prisoner of war camp.

"What I don't understand is why the army never contacted us directly," said Mr Farquhar, "and why it was Eunice here who brought us a letter written by Duncan."

Gus glanced at Eunice. He had conveniently failed to mention that Duncan was working as an SOE agent and was wearing civilian clothes at the time he broke his leg. He hadn't told them about swapping his own RAF uniform for Duncan's French-style civvies and furiously breaking free Duncan's dog-tags, so as to prevent his friend from being shot as a spy. When captured, Duncan had claimed to be Flight Lieutenant Gustaw Springer, RAF. Any news about Duncan went not to his parents, but to whatever squadron Gus was posted to. Duncan, meanwhile, had written care of Eunice so that she might explain the situation.

"That's the forces for you, Mr Farquhar," smiled Eunice, "always getting things mixed up."

"It's the confusion of war, I'm afraid, sir," added Gus.

"All very regrettable," said Mr Farquhar. "Aye, very regrettable indeed."

Gus had finished his tea. "Oh my, look at the time. I really must get back."

"Are you still at Elvington?" asked Eunice.

"Yes, but don't try to contact me there. I'm about to move back to Tempsford. Back to flying in Lysanders. If you need to pass on any information about what we've been discussing, use this number." He gave her a piece of paper with a London phone number and Detective Inspector Ruskin's name on it.

CHAPTER 24

Gus's official departure from Elvington was underwhelming to say the least. There was no dining out. Few of those bright Free French officers he had met six weeks ago were still there. None of those who were turned up to see him off. There was no fond farewell.

He didn't expect it. This was war. Officers came and went. Some were dead. Nobody seemed to care. Pascal Pascale had been promoted and had moved on. Xavier Monet was now a sous-lieutenant but was away on a training course. Izzy Parry had been given a transfer to another base. *Probably to get away from me*, thought Gus. Who could blame her?

It was a different WAAF driver that took him to York station. Carrying a small canvas and leather bag which contained spare clothes for a couple of days away, and his gas mask case, Gus clambered aboard the London train. Most of his kit had already been sent on to Tempsford, but Gus had a couple of days before he resumed his SOE flying and he had other work to do.

His first task was to meet Detective Inspector Ruskin in that same pub near South Kensington underground station. It was early afternoon by the time he got there, and Ruskin was waiting for him. He was sitting by a window, smoking a cigarette, a half-consumed pint of ale in front of him.

"You're a bit late, but good to see you all the same," said Ruskin, with a smile.

"Train was delayed. Don't get up," said Gus. "I'll get myself a drink. You want another?"

"Better not. I'm on duty, officially."

Gus soon returned with a double whisky.

"How did it go with your ex-fiancée?" asked Ruskin.

"She's on board. She's trying to track Baudouin and Claude down as we speak. She's going to meet me the day after tomorrow, and I've given her your number."

"Good. I've got the diary."

"Did you find anything in it? Anything about the Dieppe report?"

"I did, as a matter of fact. Here, I have it with me. Thought you might like to have a read." Ruskin handed Grindlethorpe's diary to Gus. "Start near the end — the last two entries."

Tuesday, 29th September 1942

A difficult day. Still dissecting Operation Jubilee. I couldn't believe ridiculous headline in the Mirror at the time: Big Hun Losses in 9-hr Dieppe Battle. That bloody Red rag never got the facts right, did it? Dieppe was a bloody disaster. And now Dickie and his people are spinning the line that Jubilee went according to plan, more or less, and is providing us with vital lessons for the future. Nonsense!

After work I walked home via the usual route. Bloody blackout was a nuisance. I suppose there's still the risk of German raids, but there haven't been any raids for months. I hate the blackout. There's no doubt it contributes to increased crime. The blackout is the pickpocket's best friend, and that so and so murderer — Gordon Cummins, the Blackout Killer. Bad that he turned out to be RAF.

As I crossed Marylebone Road to enter those quieter, cobbled streets north of it, between the railway station and Regent's Park, I had the sudden feeling that I was being followed. I stopped. All was silent. Had I heard something behind me? No. But there it was again. Footsteps on the cobblestones. I stopped and turned to my left so that I could cross the road and take a good look at the street behind me. There was nothing to be seen.

"Interesting that the papers are still talking about Dieppe. Who's Dickie?" asked Ruskin when Gus looked up.

"Mountbatten. He was in overall command."

"Of course. Read on."

Wednesday, 30th September 1942

I heard it again tonight. That same bloody sound behind me. Somebody was there in the darkness, following me. I'm sure of it. Once I stopped, looked around and shouted, "Who's there?"

A cat strolled across the street and settled itself in a doorway on the opposite side. You're getting nervous, Titus old boy, I thought. You think somebody has it in for you. Made too many enemies on your path through this bloody war. Come on, man. Be sensible. Who would bear a grudge against you?

What about Beaumont? He's never liked me. The feeling's mutual, of course. He blames me for the death of Stewart Poore in Malta. Thinks I was after him. Both are utter nonsense. Yes, I gave the ack-ack team at Ta Kali the order to fire. That doesn't make me responsible for Poore's death. The crew were aiming at the bloody Italian bomber and anyway, vast amounts of ack-ack we fired never hit anything. It was an accident of war. Nothing more. Did I think Beaumont's Hurricane was the one closing in on the Italian bomber? I had no bloody idea.

Or maybe it's that other bloody Pole, Krawiec. I wonder if he still suspects me of undermining Operation Lodz? I didn't, but Krawiec is a nasty piece of work, and he could put one of the Polish SOE thugs onto me.

Peacock has never liked me. He was always puzzled by how much money I have. None of his business. He's too old to go following people around in the blackout, anyway.

A member of that blasted French cell? They knew they'd sent a report and maybe found out that no Lysanders had been lost. If so, they'd assume the report had reached Blighty. Perhaps they suspected someone in London tipped off the Gestapo? But they'd never pin that on me, would they? They've never heard of me, unless Beaumont said something, that is. Or Eunice bloody Hesketh.

What about Farquhar? Could it be him? Impossible — he's banged up in a Germany POW camp. Or is he? Has the bastard escaped a second time?

"You told me most of this already, Guv," said Gus, moving to hand the diary back to Ruskin.

"Nice to see it written in his own hand, though. Now, have a look at the entry for the thirty-first of August."

Gus thumbed back to find the relevant page:

Monday, 31st August 1942

I had a wonderful, late breakfast in Russell Square this morning. Lovely, orange-yolked eggs and I just don't know where they get the sausages.

The papers are still going on about Dieppe, still heralding it as a success, of course. Pity it went so badly. All those Canadians dead. The tanks. The RAF lost over a hundred aeroplanes and sixty-four crew. I sometimes wonder whether it would have been better if I had passed the report on to Peacock. It's safe, the report. I met the pilot at Tangmere and debriefed him personally. I read it, thoroughly, and dismissed it. Total exaggeration. A work of fiction by a bunch of Reds in a Resistance cell intent on turning post-war France into a Communist state.

Gus handed the diary back to Ruskin. "So Grindlethorpe was a bloody traitor."

"Or a patriot who thought he was protecting the country," offered Ruskin.

"Do you believe that?"

"Doesn't matter what I believe. Facts are facts. Grindlethorpe concealed the report, as some people suspected he had. It doesn't get us anywhere nearer to finding his killer." Ruskin paused to light up another cigarette. "What about Mr Krawiec? How's that progressing, Gus?"

"I'm heading up to Essex tomorrow."

"Is he expecting you?"

"No. It was too difficult to arrange a pretext in advance. Anyway, I decided it might be better to take him by surprise. I found out that he's there at the moment, not away on a job or anything, I mean. But it might be my bad luck that he isn't there tomorrow. We'll just have to take that chance."

"Good," said Ruskin. "Very good. I'm optimistic."

"If you don't mind me asking, Guv, what does your office think you are up to?"

"Up to? Well, they don't know anything about this little ongoing investigation, if that's what you mean. No. This is between you, me and Miss Hesketh. As far as my office knows, I'm investigating a criminal gang that's forging ration books."

"Ration books?"

"Did you know that a black-market ration book sells for five pounds? Five pounds — that's close to a week's wages for many people. Some are stolen, of course. But I'm onto a gang using underground printers. Before the war they'd have been producing dirty pictures — you know the sort?"

"I can guess."

"But now they've found that forged ration books and clothing coupons sell even better." Ruskin finished his beer. "That reminds me, I'd better be off. Work to do." He stood to go. "Bloody cold outside," he went on. "Not good for my cough. Must get myself a scarf and some gloves."

"You need to stop smoking, Guv. Good luck with the forgery gang."

"Thank you, and good luck with Krawiec. Keep me posted, won't you?"

"I'm in London for a few days. I'll call you if there's anything to report."

Gus needed somewhere to stay. He could get a train to Winchester, of course, but that was too far out of town to be useful and he'd have to explain himself to the staff.

He could pay a visit to his cousin, Staś, and hope there was an available billet in the mess at RAF Hendon. There probably would be space, and he always appreciated spending time with Staś, but he didn't want to lie to him about his purpose. Alternatively, he could get a room for a couple of nights in one of the numerous bed and breakfast joints around London's main railway stations.

He chose the latter.

The boarding house was near Euston. It made for a short walk to Peacock's office if he needed to pay him a visit and was close to a couple of underground stations. The room was small and cold, but the landlady, Mrs McKenna, only charged five and sixpence, which included breakfast. Moreover, it was somewhere Gus could be completely anonymous, and that was what he wanted.

Tomorrow he would travel to Audley End to speak to Krawiec. What on earth would he say to him? He had no idea, but he decided to forget about it for now.

He ran a bath in the room off the landing. The pipes rattled, but the water was hot. He went back to his room and picked up the copy of Erskine Childers' *The Riddle of the Sands* he had begun reading in Elvington.

Relaxed though he was following his bath, hours later Gus was still tossing and turning in his bed. Sleep wouldn't come. Again, he wondered if he should seek out some medical advice.

CHAPTER 25

Gus carried an old leather briefcase to Audley End house. It wasn't unusual for documents to be hand-delivered from the Special Operations Executive HQ to SOE outposts by courier. Nothing so secret could be sent via Royal Mail. The only unusual thing about the delivery Gus was making today was that this briefcase was empty. For Gus to arrive at Audley End unannounced and simply ask to see Krawiec would have been out of order. He'd never get past the sentries.

But the briefcase, and bluff, might just get him inside.

As he climbed out of the taxi and paid the driver, Gus glanced towards the gates. On guard at the entrance lodge was a stern-looking soldier with Polish insignia on his battledress.

"Flight Lieutenant Beaumont to see Squadron Leader Krawiec," he said, showing his ID.

The sentry deferred to an NCO, who came out of the guard room office and saluted.

"Flight Lieutenant Beaumont to see Squadron Leader Krawiec," repeated Gus.

"Wait here, please," said the corporal in heavily accented English. He marched off back to the guard room. After a few minutes, he returned. "I am sorry, sir. There is nothing in the squadron leader's diary."

"Then there must be some mistake," said Gus, switching to fluent Polish. "My orders are to meet with Squadron Leader Krawiec personally and hand these documents to him." He waved the briefcase as though it contained a package of vitally important dispatches. "Nobody else, understand? Now, telephone the Squadron Leader's office immediately and explain that Flight Lieutenant Beaumont is here to see him."

The NCO couldn't refuse. All now depended on Krawiec's reaction. Five minutes later, a soldier was escorting Gus to a large house on the base, up a flight of stairs and into a large office.

"Gustaw Beaumont, nice to see you again. I wasn't expecting you."

"No, sir," said Gus. "I admit to bending the rules a little. I need to speak to you. Confidentially."

"About what?"

"About Squadron Leader Grindlethorpe's death."

"What? What on earth has that got to do with either of us?"

"And Operation Lodz."

"Tragic, wasn't it?"

"Which, sir?"

"Both, I suppose."

"Any further news about Lodz? What went wrong there?"

"That matter has absolutely nothing to do with you, Beaumont. But no. No, there isn't, as a matter of fact. And Grindlethorpe's death? What do you want to know about that?"

"I wondered what you thought about it, sir. You see, before the RAF Police began its investigation, a civilian officer interviewed me about it. I was a suspect. I need to clear my name."

"I see."

"This detective was under the impression that the killer may have been somebody known to Grindlethorpe."

"Someone like me?"

"He didn't mention any names," lied Gus, "but I remember what you said when we were debriefed on the Lodz mission. That you…"

"That I'd kill Grindlethorpe if I found he'd betrayed the operation?"

"Yes. That, and the fact that you believed he had betrayed Lodz."

"You're right. I still think he did betray us," said Krawiec, a look of disgust on his face. "You seem to have turned into an amateur sleuth."

Gus smiled and waited for more.

"If you must know, I spent the whole of September and October in Canada. I was supervising an SOE training establishment there — let's simply call it Camp X, and by the way, this is top secret. Understand, Beaumont?"

"I understand."

"As it happens, I read about Grindlethorpe's death whilst in Canada. We received British newspapers. Later, of course. As I say, tragic business. But not nearly so tragic as what happened on Operation Lodz."

Had either the RAF Police or Detective Inspector Ruskin still been actively investigating the murder, they would have sought verification of Krawiec's version of events. Gus, on the other hand, had only Krawiec's say so and his own instinct to go on.

"Would you like coffee?" asked Krawiec.

Gus needed to get back to London and prepare for the next phase of the investigation. On the other hand, Krawiec might give more away if he relaxed a little.

"Coffee would be nice, thank you."

Krawiec ordered coffee to be brought through to his office. "I take it you've been busy, Beaumont?"

"Yes, sir. I've just completed a spell away from SOE piloting. Been with a Free French heavy bomber unit up in Yorkshire."

"And how are those French doing?"

"They're doing all right." There was no need to elaborate.

"It's interesting, isn't it, that we are all here? The French, the Dutch, the Czechs — and us, the Poles, of course. All here in London, fighting the Nazis. I can see why the British and Americans are keen to support a Free French bomber unit."

"Why is that?"

"Because pretty soon the Allies will have to start dropping bombs on France, and when they do, it will be better if they can say French forces are involved too."

Gus simply nodded. Krawiec was right, of course.

"You say you've finished that posting?"

"That's right. I'm on my way back to Tempsford the day after tomorrow."

"And Sir Alex asked you to bring some papers to me?" he asked, looking at the briefcase.

"Oh, that. No, sir. The briefcase is empty. I apologise. Wing Commander Peacock knows nothing about this; I'm acting alone to clear my name. You see, although the RAF are not interested in me, I have a feeling the civilian police may still think I did it."

"Did you do it?"

"No."

A knock at the office door. The coffee had arrived. An orderly poured for them both, then left.

"And you say a civilian police officer interviewed you about Grindlethorpe's death?"

"That's correct."

"Nobody came to see me."

"No. As I say, they think I did it — I'm pretty sure I was the only one to be questioned before the RAF Police took over. They've put the case on ice. Closed it, really. They're sure it's a random killing. A thief after an officer's wallet and prepared to cosh him to get it."

"That makes sense. The blackout makes it easy, I suppose."

"My thoughts exactly, sir."

"I wonder why the RAF investigators took over? I'd have thought it a civilian case."

"No idea, sir."

Krawiec took a long sip of coffee. "Ghastly stuff isn't?" he said, not waiting for an answer. "How is your cousin? Rosen?"

"He's very well, sir, thank you. Though the squadron is suffering attrition, as you'd expect. I don't suppose it's the easiest thing to do, writing to family, I mean."

"No. That can't be easy."

Soon, with their coffee finished and their conversation over, it was time to go. Gus thanked Krawiec for his time, picked up the briefcase and departed. He left Audley End convinced that Krawiec was being truthful. He'd been nowhere near England, let alone London, on the night Grindlethorpe had been killed. Moreover, he seemed as mystified as the rest of them as to why the RAF had taken on the investigation.

From a telephone box in Euston, Gus rang Ruskin.

"Anything to report?"

"I'm back from seeing Krawiec. Can we meet?"

"It will have to be tomorrow. And listen, Miss Hesketh has called me. She's heading down, too. Time to meet up as a team?"

Gus had been thinking of where best to meet Eunice when the time came. The Greek Street tearoom they used to frequent was simply out of the question. He'd settled on the

Royal Geographical Society building. Now Ruskin would be there too. He was right; it was time they met up as a team. If it became necessary, Ruskin could keep the peace between them.

"Lowther Lodge, after lunch. Two o'clock?"

"Yes, I'll be there. Miss Hesketh will telephone when she arrives in London. I'll tell her where and when."

Gus needed to begin thinking about questioning the Frenchmen, Baudouin and Claude. That, he thought uncomfortably, meant confronting Eunice again. For now, it was back to Mrs McKenna's boarding house in Euston. Once again, he'd try for a decent night's sleep.

CHAPTER 26

Gus didn't know when he'd decided that he must see a doctor, but he was determined to do it today. His insomnia was proving to be a bigger problem than he'd ever imagined.

By rights, of course, he ought to have sought advice from the RAF doctor on base. But Gus worried his symptoms wouldn't be taken seriously. A military medic would very likely think he was shirking, trying to avoid going into the air. Or worse, they might take him too seriously and ground him. Neither of these outcomes appealed.

He could try Harris, the elderly doctor in Winchester who had cared for both his parents up until their deaths. But he didn't have the inclination to trot over to Hampshire. There must be somebody he knew here in London.

Gus got up and had a quick wash using cold water, which was all Mrs McKenna seemed to be able to supply in the mornings. He put on his uniform and went downstairs to the tiny basement room, where the landlady served breakfast.

He wracked his brain as he ate his bowl of thin porridge. Nothing. Then, whilst finishing the last piece of toast smothered in margarine, it came to him. Barnaby Curruthers.

He'd been friendly with Barney at Oxford; they'd played rugby together for the college team. Barney was a little older than Gus and was studying medicine. He'd qualified as a doctor at the same time that Gus had graduated.

Barney was a conscientious objector, and when war was declared in 1939 he had refused to join up. Not that this mattered to Gus. He held no resentment towards Barney, who was free to have his own principles and stick to them. In fact, he rather respected Barney for having the courage to do so — wasn't that what they were fighting for? Personal liberties and free speech? Anyway, doctors were needed in civilian hospitals just as badly as they were needed on the front line in the North African desert or in military hospitals here at home.

Now, where was it that Barney worked? Gus struggled to recall for a few moments before it came to him: St Thomas' Hospital in Lambeth. Not too far away at all, but was he still working there?

Gus headed out. He walked south, across Bloomsbury, heading down towards the Thames. St Thomas' Hospital was easy to find, just over the bridge at Westminster. For a while Gus simply loitered around the main entrance, hoping to spot his friend. It was futile. Eventually he went inside, looked around and spotted the reception desk.

"Excuse me," he said to a middle-aged woman sitting behind the desk, her head bent over a stack of papers, "I'm looking for Doctor Carruthers. Please could you tell me if he's on duty at the moment?"

"Can I ask what it's about?" she asked, without looking up.

"Doctor Carruthers is an old chum of mine, from university. We've not seen each other for years. The war, you know? Anyway, I've got some news for him, about a friend of ours."

"And you are, sir?" she asked, eyes pinned to her lists.

"Flight Lieutenant Gus Beaumont."

The woman looked up and took in his uniform. Her face changed, breaking into a wide smile. "I'll see what I can find out for you, dear. Just wait over there, would you?" She pointed to a row of chairs placed opposite the reception desk. Gus sat down.

Eventually, after what felt like hours, she returned. "Doctor Carruthers will see you, Flight Lieutenant. Please follow me."

The woman led Gus through a main corridor, up a flight of stairs and into a small office. There was a distinct smell about the place, a mix of antiseptic and floor polish.

They reached an office on the second floor and the woman showed him in. Gus found Barney Carruthers sitting behind a desk, scrutinising some documents. He looked up. "Gus Beaumont. What a surprise! Good to see you."

"Good to see you, too, Barney."

"Thank you, Mrs Johnson," said Barney, looking at the receptionist. The woman left the office and he turned to Gus. "So, what brings you here?"

"I wanted to see you in a professional capacity, actually."

"Did you? Go on then."

Gus explained his insomnia. "What can I do, Barney?" he asked. "I've been taking Cassell's tablets for a few weeks. Two tablets three times a day, as it says on the jar."

"And?"

"Not touching me."

"I'm not surprised. Quack medicine."

"That's why I'm asking you. I need something stronger. Something that will work. What do you suggest, Barney?"

"You could drink yourself into a stupor."

"Tried that, no luck."

"Or —" Barney paused to take a small bottle from a shelf at the side of the office — "you can pop one of these. Half an hour before going to bed — see if it helps. Better than knock-out drops, and so much better than Dr Cassell's."

"What are they?"

"Phenobarbital," said Barney. "Give them a try. They can't do any harm."

"How much?" he asked.

"As you're a serving RAF officer, and as we're friends, give me a ten-bob note, but don't let on to anyone."

Gus took a note from his wallet and handed it to Barney. "Thank you," he said.

"What are you up to these days, Gus? Specifically, I mean."

"Can't be too specific — walls have ears and all that. Suffice to say I'm between postings at the moment. Couple of days off."

"Still seeing that Hesketh girl?"

"No. Haven't seen Eunice for years," Gus lied. "What are you up to, Barney?"

"I'm off back to Oxford. Next week, as a matter of fact. I've been seconded to an Australian research doctor. Pathologist called Florey. He and his team are working on penicillin."

"What's that?"

"It's a naturally occurring substance, a sort of mould, I suppose you'd say. Seems it can destroy bacteria. Florey's team have isolated the active ingredients and have carried out some limited trials. Seems it works. This could be a world-changer, Gus. We could see it wiping out infections. Anyway, the team are about to go into large-scale medical trials and I'm going up there to help. Very exciting."

"Sounds it. Well, must be off, Barney," said Gus, standing and offering his hand. "Thanks ever so much for the help. Good luck with the new job."

"And you, Gus. And you."

Gus was halfway through the door when Barney called him back.

"Just one other thing, Gus, old man," he said. "Don't go too heavy on the Scotch with those things, eh? And no more than one a day."

From the hospital Gus crossed Westminster Bridge. The chimes from Big Ben rang out as he entered the tube station. One o'clock. He'd better get over to Lowther Lodge.

CHAPTER 27

Gus took the circle line to South Kensington. Though the day was chill, throughout the whole journey he felt the sweat on his brow and found himself mopping it with a handkerchief. From South Kensington tube station he walked up Exhibition Road towards Hyde Park and Lowther Lodge. Once there, he waited at reception.

Gus saw Eunice approaching the main entrance and smiled. She was wearing a light grey macintosh with a matching hat. She carried a brown leather handbag and matching brown shoes. Gus looked at her face. Did she seem happier than when he last saw her? Hard to tell, but still she offered him no smile.

Gus walked over towards her, uncertain of what to say. He offered a hand, which she took. It was a nervous handshake, her grip weak.

"DI Ruskin isn't here yet," he said, in a businesslike manner. "Let's get you signed in, then we can sit down. Someone will tell us once he arrives. Let me take your coat."

She allowed Gus to help her off with her coat. Underneath, she was wearing a royal blue, two-piece outfit. They walked silently along a corridor and into the meeting room, where they sat down.

"Good journey?" asked Gus.

"Yes, not too bad. It's a long way, obviously."

"Still reading *Chimneys*?"

"Yes. Nearly finished it."

"Eunice, I just wanted to…"

The door swung open. "Your other visitor is here, Flight Lieutenant Beaumont," said the receptionist.

Excellent bloody timing, thought Gus, as he returned to reception with the woman. The detective was standing there expectantly. "Is she here yet?"

"Yes," Gus replied. "Come on, Guv. Let's get on with it."

As they entered the small meeting room, Ruskin moved towards Eunice. "You must be Miss Hesketh," he said, offering his hand. "Delighted to meet you, and thank you very much for coming along."

"Eunice, please, if you don't mind."

"And I'm Detective Inspector Sam Ruskin. Most people refer to me as the Governor, or Guv. I'll start, shall I?"

"Go ahead, Guv."

"Has Gus told you what we're up against? What all this is about?"

"Yes, he has."

"Gus has been to see Mr Krawiec and, with your help, Eunice, we are hoping to track down these French agents. You've started working on it, apparently. Have you found anything about the whereabouts of the Frenchmen?"

"Yes. It seems they've been split up. The younger one, Claude, is down at Beaulieu being prepared to be dropped back into France on some special operation. We'll have to be quick if we're going to talk to him."

"It won't be easy," said Gus. "If Claude is being prepared for a drop, he'll be out of circulation. Only cleared people will be able to see him."

"I wonder if that might be another job for you, Eunice?" said Ruskin. "You were tasked with working with their group; I expect you'll know the drill. Besides, you may come across as more non-threatening. Lull them into a sense of security. What do you think?"

"You're right," said Gus. "Eunice, you can go to see Peacock. Ask if you can meet Claude for old time's sake and brief him at the same time. You know all about drops and pick-ups."

"Will the Wing Commander buy that?"

"He might," said Gus. "Are you happy to give it a try?"

"Yes. Nothing to lose. The worst Peacock can do is say no."

"Good," said Ruskin. "Now, tell us about the other character."

"Baudouin. Luckily, he's also close by," Eunice continued. "He's with General de Gaulle's staff here in London, at their headquarters on Carlton Gardens. We've more time with him, but they're talking about relocating to North Africa at the earliest opportunity, so we can't leave it too long."

"We can't leave anything too long," said Ruskin, a melancholy expression on his face. Then he started coughing. Eunice gave him a handkerchief and eventually the hacking cough stopped.

"Sorry about that," he said. "I suggest you tackle Claude as soon as possible, then Baudouin immediately afterwards."

"Good plan," said Gus. "There's time for Eunice to see Peacock today."

"Now, Gus, how did you get on with Mr Krawiec?"

"It went according to plan. I got into the place and he was there; that was my biggest worry out of the way. I told him I was under suspicion for killing Grindlethorpe, and he opened up. He owned up to blaming Grindlethorpe for what happened on the Lodz mission; Krawiec still believes he sold us out. But he has a sound alibi for the time of the murder."

"What is it?"

"He was in Canada for two months. All of September and October."

"Well, that seems to put him in the clear. All very good work," said Ruskin. "Now, I can see you two have some planning to do, so I'll be off. As you say, see Peacock and that younger French fellow as soon as possible. We don't want to lose him." With that, he departed, leaving Gus and Eunice in an awkward silence.

"That's a wicked cough he's got," Eunice said eventually.

"Yes. Seems to be getting worse. Look, Eunice, are you sure you're all right about being involved in this?"

"Yes, of course. I'll go over to Baker Street as soon as we're through. But how are we going to go about asking Claude and Baudouin for information once we get to see them?"

"Softly, softly, catchee monkey, Eunice."

"What?"

"You know, the old saying. We'll take a patient and cautious approach to achieve our goal."

She looked at him quizzically.

"Don't worry. We'll just ask them." He thought he detected a smile at that. "It's almost three," he went on. "We need to make a plan. Do you want to stay here, or go somewhere else?"

"A bit of fresh air would be good. Then could we pop in somewhere for a bite to eat? Tea?"

"Well, it's a bit early, but I'm sure we'll find somewhere. Shall we walk across the park and then find somewhere around Lancaster Gate? Does that sound all right?"

"Yes."

They strolled across the park, along the edge of the Serpentine. The water looked cold and uninviting.

"How are Duncan's parents?"

"They're coping. His mother is finding the whole thing wearing, I think. Father's doing better. It helped that you were able to tell them a bit about Duncan's capture. It must be a strain on them."

"The whole war's a strain on all of us. I've had a bad few weeks, to be honest. Months even. Eunice, if I'm honest with you, and I want to be, I think that's why I…"

"Oh my God, Gus. Look at that!"

He followed her gaze. A group of four-engined aircraft flew over them, their silver paintwork reflecting the weak rays of the November sun.

"Are they German?" Eunice asked.

"No. They're US Airforce bombers. B-17s. Flying Fortresses, the Yanks call them. They must be coming back from a daylight raid."

"Daylight bombing? It won't work, will it?"

"No. Not without long-range fighter escort, and we don't have them. None of our fighters have the range, and the Yanks have nothing."

"So how do they expect to defend themselves?"

"Close formation and lots of machine guns creating a crossfire. The idea is that firepower will keep German fighters away."

"Does it work?"

"I doubt it. Look at those poor buggers — they've suffered a bit of a savaging."

Eunice looked again at the aeroplanes. Gus was right. There weren't many of them; they must have suffered losses. Those that had survived showed signs of having taken a beating. There was damage to the tailplane of one, and another seemed to be running on just three engines, smoke billowing from the fourth.

"Those poor men," she said.

They walked on and found a café that was serving high teas.

"Meat paste sandwiches," Eunice said, with a frown.

"There's a war on, I'll remind you," Gus replied with a smile.

He didn't like the silences between their idle chit-chat. It seemed that things weren't going too well.

"I'd better be off to see Sir Alex," said Eunice, once she'd finished eating.

"Come back here and tell me how it went?"

"Not here. A pub, maybe?"

"All right. There's a place on University Road in Bloomsbury. Don't remember its name, but it's the only one there."

"I'll find it," she said, handing him a half crown. "This is for the food."

"No it's all right. This is on me."

"I'd rather chip in, if you don't mind."

Once she'd gone, Gus settled the bill and then wandered over to Bloomsbury. He picked up an evening paper. It was getting dark now, but the streets were busy with office workers beginning to make their way home. Eventually he found the pub, the Duke of Wellington. It was crowded; nobody would think there was a war on. With difficulty, he wove his way to the bar.

"What can I get you, darlin'?" asked the barmaid.

Gus looked at the array of labels on the hand pumps. Most pubs had a straightforward choice of bitter or mild. Here there were five different beers on tap.

"You've got me there," he said. "Can you talk me through them, please?"

She started with the first pump, the one to his left. "This is a bitter. It's very light and refreshing, but not terribly strong.

More of a summer drink, in my opinion, but many folks like it at all times of year. Next, we have our best bitter. It's a darker, almost red-coloured ale, and stronger, it being 'best'. Then we have the mild. It's a dark mild, mind, and much stronger than you'd think. Has a bit of a reputation for making folk fight. Next is the porter, black as coal but not that strong, somewhere between the bitter and best bitter. And last but not least is our winter warmer: a strong, dark brown ale, which we only serve in half pints. What can I get you?"

"I think I'll go for a pint of the porter, please."

"A good choice," she said. "And would you like a handle or a tall hat?"

"Beg your pardon?"

She brought two glasses from behind the bar. "You can have a pint glass tankard with a handle like this one, or a straight glass like this. Tall hats, we call them."

"Does it matter?"

"Depends how fast you're going to drink the beer, darlin'. If you're going to down your pint quickly, I'd go for the tall hat. But if you want to sit a while and linger, then the tankard will keep it cooler for longer. Personal preference too, of course."

"Well, I've brought a paper and I'm meeting someone later, so I'll go for the handle, please."

She took the glass, placed it under the tap and began pulling on the pump, which sent streams of black liquid into the pint pot. As the beer settled, Gus looked at the perfect contrast between the black porter and the light froth that formed on its surface. He settled down to read the paper and wait.

Eunice arrived exactly an hour and two pints later.

"Was Peacock there?" Gus asked.

"Yes."

"And?"

"Get me a drink, would you? Gin and tonic, please."

"Not sure you'll get the tonic here; it's a bit of a spit and sawdust place. Sorry."

"It's all right. Just get me something. I'm so thirsty, and this smoke doesn't help."

Gus went to the bar and reappeared with two glasses: gin and soda for her, and half a winter warmer for himself.

"It went well," said Eunice, taking a sip of her drink. "I've managed to persuade the wing commander to let me conduct part of Claude's briefing."

"Was he suspicious?"

"No, I don't think so. He said we can go down there early next week, but no later than Wednesday."

"Hold on. We?"

"Yes. He thinks you can brief Claude on drop-off procedure."

"Did Peacock suggest that?"

"No. I told him Claude trusts you, and that you'd be useful. Peacock's given me the papers we'll need to gain admittance."

"You've done well, Eunice."

"So, we'll go to see him next week. Monday?"

"Yes. I'm back at Tempsford on Saturday, but I'm sure I'll be able to wangle Monday off. There's not a full moon for a fortnight."

"When we do meet him, remember, Claude knows me as Clairice. They both do. We can leave it at that."

"Agreed. That's for the best."

Once they'd finished their drinks, Gus asked where she was staying.

"Hampstead. I thought I'd use the flat."

"I can walk you there, if you like."

"There's no need."

"I'd feel better if I did."

"I said there's no need, Gus."

"As you wish. We'll go down to question Claude in Hampshire next Monday. We can take a train from Waterloo to Brockenhurst. I'll meet you at the station. Is nine o'clock all right?"

"Yes. That's fine. Goodbye for now, Gus."

She shook his hand. Was her grip just a little firmer this time?

"Goodbye, Eunice."

Gus had a couple more pints in the pub, then went to the RAF Club for tea. He was due back at Tempsford the following day but had to face a final night in his room at Mrs McKenna's lodging house. Once there, he got ready for bed and popped one of the phenobarbital pills, remembering too late that Barney had told him not to drink too much alcohol with them.

That night, for the first time in what seemed like years, he slept like a baby.

CHAPTER 28

The following day, Gus travelled back to Tempsford and received a warm welcome form his friends. "I want to unpack and then take one of the Lizzies up for a spin," he said. "I'm already feeling rusty. Are any of them ready to fly?"

"C for Charlie has just had a full engine overhaul and needs testing," said Doggie. "Up for it?"

"You bet I'm up for it, Doggie. Just try stopping me."

"All right then. I'll check with the mechanics that she's ready to go up."

Half an hour later, Gus was sitting in the cockpit of the Lysander, taxiing to the eastern end of the strip. Once the affirmative message had been received from the control tower, he opened up the throttle and listened as the engine roared. Brakes off, the Lysander gathered pace along the Tempsford runway and quickly gained take-off speed. He pulled back on the stick and up she went, soaring high into the sky.

Gus steered southwest. This took him over Bletchley and he glanced down at the huts in the grounds of the big house. Bunty had worked there until that blasted Fw-190 Jabo had dropped its bomb on them in Hastings. Working at Bletchley Park was Eunice's cover story back here in Blighty. Gus had never been there and was unlikely to ever do so, since it was top secret.

He turned to starboard and took a north-westerly course that led to Warwick. He circled over the city, then Coventry and Leicester. From there it was south-southeast to Northampton and on to Bletchley.

RAF Tempsford was to the east of Bletchley Park, but that was downwind. Gus overshot the base and flew on to Cambridge, where he turned into wind to prepare for landing.

It was then that the engine cut out.

The correct approach speed in a glide or throttled off was eighty miles per hour. Gus looked at the speedometer. The aircraft was doing ninety but beginning to lose speed as it flew into wind. Gus knew that the Lysander had a stalling speed of less than sixty miles per hour. She was very unlikely to stall, but if she did a wing would drop and a slow right-hand spiral would commence.

He shut off the ignition and fuel supply, fully wound back the tail actuating gear and pushed the nose of the Lysander down. In this manner, he found he could glide at eighty, making a slow descent towards the Tempsford landing strip.

"Tempsford Control, this is C for Charlie, repeat C for Charlie, over."

"C for Charlie, this is Control. What's up, Bouncer?"

"Engine's packed up on me. Preparing for forced landing, over."

"Understood. I'll make sure the strip remains clear for you. Good luck, over."

"Thanks, Control. C for Charlie out."

Gus saw an RAF fire tender race out to the strip, closely followed by an ambulance. Good to know they were mobilised, he supposed.

The flaps on the Lysander were automatically controlled by slats on the leading edge of the wing, and at a normal approach speed of eighty miles per hour the flaps were about halfway down. As the Lizzie slowed yet more, with Gus keeping her nose up, the flaps came down almost fully.

Soon he was over the strip and had the Lysander flared for a three-point landing. As the speed fell, Gus pulled back on the stick and the Lizzie landed perfectly. Rather than apply the brakes, he left the Lysander to come to a halt at the windward end of the runway. He opened the cowling grills and adjusted the tail trim for take-off, as normal. As he clambered down from the cockpit, sweat pouring from his brow, a tractor came out to tow the disabled Lysander back to the service hangar.

I need a drink, thought Gus. He almost ran over to the mess.

"What would you like, sir?" asked the orderly behind the bar.

"Whisky Mac. A large one, please. Just the one cube of ice."

"So, you had a bit of bother up there," said Doggie, seated in an armchair by the fire.

"Yes, you could say that." Gus wiped his brow.

"Unusual. They're very reliable engines. Something not done properly in the service, I expect."

"Well, you'd better find out. Somebody needs a rollocking, to make sure they don't make the same mistake again."

"Here you are, sir," said the barman.

Gus looked at the glass of Scotch, the single ice cube and the half bottle of dry ginger ale beside it.

"That's not a bloody Whisky Mac. Whisky Mac is Scotch and green ginger wine. Everyone knows that."

"Oh, sorry, sir. It's what I've always called a Whisky Mac."

"Well, you're wrong, I'm afraid. Put it right, will you?"

"Yes, sir. Straight away."

"Come and sit down, Bouncer, old boy. And calm down," said Doggie, blowing pipe tobacco smoke.

"I'll bring it over, sir."

"Thank you," said Gus, and he strolled over towards Doggie and sat on the sofa.

"You're quite right, of course. A Whisky Mac is Scotch and ginger wine. What he gave you was a Whisky Dry."

"Can't get the staff nowadays," said Gus.

"No. There's a war on, apparently. Do you know why it's called a Whisky Mac, out of interest?"

"No, I don't. Tell me."

"It's short for Whisky MacDonald. It seems that a certain Colonel Hector MacDonald first crafted the drink forty odd years ago, out in India. Lots of ginger out there, and ginger wine is supposed to be a good remedy for a host of ailments, from digestive issues to cholera. It caught on with the Brits, and MacDonald mixed it with whisky."

"You are a font of knowledge, Doggie. So, what about the Whisky Dry?"

"Easy. During the prohibition over in the States, dry ginger ale was mixed with contraband whisky to cover up the smell of the alcohol."

"Well, I never," said Gus, taking a sip of the correct drink the orderly had by now brought him. "Well, I know which I prefer. This."

"Now then," said Doggie, "time to tell me what you've been up to."

Gus settled down to recount his tale of working with the French and bombing Germany.

As Gus thought, it was easy to get Monday off. He travelled down to London the afternoon before and stayed again at Mrs McKenna's place. At nine he met Eunice at Waterloo station, and they took the train down to Brockenhurst in the New Forest and a taxi to Beaulieu.

Showing their passes at the gatehouse, they went through to one of the internal rooms in the main building, where Claude was waiting for them.

"Clarice! Monsieur Bouncer! *C'est un plaisir de te revoir.* They told me you'll help with my final briefing. I'm pleased about that because I trust you both. It'll be easier to ask questions and speak openly about things I might not disclose to others."

"Such as?"

"Well, to be honest, I'll admit that I'm frightened."

"That's perfectly natural," said Eunice.

"Frightened of anything in particular?" asked Gus.

"The landing. That aeroplane you came over in was an absolute mess when it crashed and caught fire. And the pilot was killed, wasn't he?"

"That was extreme bad luck," said Gus. "Things like that are very, very rare. This time it will be a Lysander. One pilot will fly and navigate the craft, with only yourself as passenger. They are very safe aeroplanes."

"But nothing is safe if the enemy are there waiting!"

"They won't be," insisted Gus.

"You're going to make your way to Paris. You have your cover ID? Your cover story?" asked Eunice.

"Yes."

"Talk us through it."

"I'm Robert Escoffier. I'm seventeen, a farmer's son from Picardy. I'm in Paris trying to find my aunt, Madame Helene Auclair. My mother died recently and my father — Madame Auclair's brother — has turned to drink. The farm is going to rack and ruin. I want her to return with me to talk some sense into the old man."

"Why don't you simply write a letter or telephone?"

"I've tried. Nothing. She's somehow run to earth."

"And you think you'll find her just by walking around Paris?"

"Of course not. My extended family are there too. I have the address of a cousin. Here." He passed a slip of paper to Eunice. It contained the name of Louis Escoffier and an address in the eleventh arrondissement.

"Nice part of town," said Eunice, looking to Gus for support.

"I'm convinced," said Gus.

"Claude," said Eunice, "how old are you actually?"

"I'm eighteen."

"You'll do well," she told him. "I'm not going to ask you about the operation."

"No," said Gus. "The fewer who know, the better."

"But we do want to talk to you about something else," said Eunice.

"Squadron Leader Titus Grindlethorpe — does that name mean anything to you?" asked Gus.

"No. Should it?"

"He's dead," said Eunice. "Murdered."

"And?"

Gus took the plunge. "Claude, please can you tell us where you were on Thursday the first and Friday the second of October? What you were doing, who you were with. Everything. It's important, Claude."

The young Frenchman looked at them, hesitating. "I ... I don't... Have you joined the police, Monsieur Bouncer?"

"No. But I'm helping them a little."

"I was travelling here. Moving from one of the SOE training bases up in Scotland. I'm sure you'd know it, but I won't give you the name, for obvious reasons..."

"We don't need the name."

"I travelled by train to Brockenhurst. I was met at the station and brought here."

"There are no through trains from Scotland to Hampshire, Claude. Where did you change?" asked Eunice.

"I came down into King's Cross. Then I took a train to Brockenhurst from Waterloo."

"Give me the times, Claude. As accurately as possible. When did you get into King's Cross?" Gus pressed.

"I think it was eight."

"That's eight o'clock on the Thursday night. Yes?"

"Approximately, yes."

"And the train to Brockenhurst?"

"Nine."

"Nine o'clock that same night?"

Claude hesitated, looking first at Eunice, then at Gus, then back again. "No. Nine the next morning."

Eunice nodded. "Where did you stay, Claude?"

"A small place near Kings Cross. A kind of pension."

"How did you spend the evening?"

"I went to Soho. Had a few drinks and a walk around. It's a lively place!"

"Did you meet anyone there? Anyone who could back up your story?" asked Gus.

"No…" Again, this followed a pause.

Gus looked at Eunice. She'd also noticed Claude's hesitation.

"You spent the evening alone?" she asked.

"That's right."

"Until what sort of time?"

"I was back in the pension shortly after midnight. The landlady saw me come in — I'm sure she'll vouch for me if necessary. But look, what is all this about?"

"I've been accused of murdering Grindlethorpe," said Gus. "I didn't do it and I'm trying to find out who did."

"And so you think I did it, Monsieur Bouncer?"

"No. No, I don't, Claude. But I'm trying to rule out as many people as I can in order to find out who did."

It was as much as they were going to get. After answering a few operational questions about his upcoming drop-off, Gus and Eunice wished Claude luck and left the SOE base, making their way back to the station at Brockenhurst.

"What do you think?" asked Gus as they sat in an otherwise empty train compartment on the way back to Waterloo.

"I think he doesn't stand a chance if the Germans get hold of him."

"I see what you mean. But regarding Grindlethorpe — do you think he's telling the truth?"

"He's hiding something, that's for sure. But I still can't believe he killed a British officer. What do you think?"

"He's telling the truth. Or at least, partly."

"Leaving something out?"

"Yes."

"About Grindlethorpe?"

"No."

"What then?"

"You noticed his hesitation and vagueness about the time he spent around Soho?"

"Yes."

"I'd say Claude was with a prostitute."

"What? Really? But, Gus, he's only eighteen!"

"He's eighteen and scared. Thinks he might be dead in a few days' time. My money's on a prostitute. Soho is a good pick-up place."

"You sound as though you're speaking from experience."

"I'm not, but your overhear things at various RAF officers' messes. Claude is innocent. Let's think about Baudouin."

"I have been thinking about him," said Eunice. "How on earth are we going get into the Free French HQ?"

"Now, that's a good question."

Gaining access would be difficult, if not impossible. Not even Wing Commander Sir Alex Peacock could wangle them into Free French HQ.

"We'll sleep on it tonight and get over to the Free French HQ tomorrow," Gus said as the train pulled into Waterloo station.

"Can you get time off? Again?"

"I'll phone the base and feign sickness. What do you suggest? Vomiting, diarrhoea, or both?"

"Say you ate something, and you've been up all night being sick. Don't overdo it. Never works."

"Shall I see you home?"

"No thanks. I can manage."

There was no point pushing her. "Where shall we meet tomorrow, then?"

"Where are you staying?"

"Near Euston."

"Meet on Gower Street? Outside Euston Square tube station?"

"What time?"

"Shall we say late morning? We can go for lunch and discuss tactics. Hopefully, one of us will have come up with an idea about getting to speak to Baudouin."

"All right, see you then. Goodnight, Eunice."

"Goodnight."

Gus walked from Waterloo across central London towards Mrs McKenna's boarding house. He thought about Soho and its grubby delights. He had money in his pocket and wondered whether he should spend some of it.

Instead, he headed straight to his room. Once there, Gus read a couple of chapters of his book and then popped a phenobarbital tablet, drank a glass of murky tap water and settled down in the small bed. Within minutes, he was fast asleep and snoring.

CHAPTER 29

The smart, well-dressed couple that walked up to the Free French Headquarters on Carlton Gardens did not look estranged from each other. Far from it. Gus wore his RAF uniform, of course, and Eunice was dressed in her light grey macintosh and matching hat, and the usual immaculate, brown leather accessories. She looked relaxed, thought Gus, as she held onto his arm. But then, he knew Eunice was a good actress. She had to be, spending months in occupied France masquerading as Clarice Delacroix.

Of course, there was no way they could get into the Free French Headquarters. But, as Gus had realised, there was no need for them to get into the HQ building. At some point, Baudouin had to come out and, when he did, they would be there waiting for him. It was simply a matter of time.

"What time do you think he finishes?"

"Absolutely no idea. Could be any time."

"We'll just have to sit it out."

Carlton Gardens was just north of St James's Park, off The Mall. The only way out was along Carlton House Terrace.

Gus and Eunice stood by the statue of Lord Curzon. This was on a plot of land where Carlton Gardens split off from Carlton House Terrace as it swung to the north, towards Pall Mall.

They took it in turns to watch out for Baudouin, sitting on a wooden bench by the statue. First, they tried to do an hour at a time, but Gus was desperate for a break after forty minutes. They decided to shorten the watch time to half an hour. It was dull, tedious work. It was also very cold.

Gus was beginning to feel that they may be wasting their time when a solitary figure walking with slight a limp came along the terrace. Eunice jumped up and broke into a trot. Yes, the man who had just come out was Baudouin.

"Baudouin, *comment ça va?*" called Eunice, and she rushed to embrace the Frenchman, kissing him on both cheeks.

Gus instantly felt a pang of jealousy. He walked over to them. "Baudouin," said Gus, "what a surprise. We were just out for a stroll."

"Really?" said the Frenchman. "Actually, I saw you here earlier, from a window. Not very good spy work, Clarice." He smiled. "Act like that in France and the Gestapo would be on you in a trice. So, you want something from me, I suppose. What is it?"

"We'll get to that later. Can we go inside somewhere? I'm so cold."

They walked over to a tearoom just down from Pall Mall and quickly found a table.

"Pot of tea for three," said Gus to a waitress.

"Coffee for me," said Baudouin. "Even bad coffee is better than that filthy stuff."

Once they had their drinks, Gus turned to the Frenchman. "You asked what we want, and I do apologise for being blunt, but can you please tell us where you were and what you were doing on the night of Thursday the first and Friday the second of October?"

"What? This sounds like a police investigation."

"It is," said Eunice.

"Sort of," added Gus. "Can you tell us, please?"

Baudouin considered this, saying nothing. *Is he stalling?* wondered Gus.

"Let me think. Where was I? I'll need to look in my diary. My memory's not so brilliant these days, I'm afraid. But you know, the fact that I can't recall indicates I wasn't doing anything particularly interesting. Why on earth do you want to know, anyway?"

"Can you check your diary?" asked Gus.

"Not now. Not here. It's at my lodgings."

"Where are they?"

"Walthamstow."

"Then we'll go with you to get it," said Eunice.

"Can't you just work out where you were?" Gus demanded.

"Calm down," Eunice urged.

"Let me sit for a while," said Baudouin, opening his briefcase and taking out a pen and notepad. He began muttering and scribbling. "*D'accord.* I have it," he eventually announced. "On Thursday I finished work in the HQ at around six. I walked from there over to Green Park metro station, stopping at a little place on Jermyn Street for something to eat. Later, I took the Victoria Line to Blackhorse Road and walked to my accommodation, which is nearby."

"And you arrived at your place at about what time?"

"I suppose it must have been after nine, no later than nine-thirty."

"I suppose you were seen leaving the HQ?"

"Yes, everyone has to sign in and out. You can check."

"No need. And the place you ate?"

"It's called the Speedy Café. Yes, they know me quite well in there."

"After you left Speedy, did anybody see you after that?" asked Gus.

"Nobody saw me. At least, nobody who might recognise me or remember me. Look, what on earth is all this about?"

"It's about the death of an RAF officer," said Gus. "We're trying to rule out people who might have wanted him out of the way."

"Who?"

"Grindlethorpe. Squadron Leader Titus Grindlethorpe. Did you know him?"

"Did I know him?" repeated Baudouin. "I don't think so."

"I'm sorry, Baudouin. It looks as if we've been rather wasting your time," said Gus. "We won't bother you again. Let's just finish our tea and go home."

As they walked away from the tearoom and Baudouin headed back towards St James's Park, Eunice asked Gus why he'd told Baudouin they wouldn't bother him again. "He doesn't have an alibi, so he's still a suspect, isn't he?"

"Do you think Baudouin killed Grindlethorpe?"

"Of course not. But that's not the way detectives work, is it?"

"We're not bloody detectives, Eunice, are we? At first, I was just trying to clear my name. Then I wondered why Scotland Yard had been taken off the Grindlethorpe murder. And why the RAF Police took over the investigation then promptly dropped it like a hot potato. I was interested. But now, I'm fed-up with it."

"It was you who wanted my help, remember? Not the other way around, so don't you get angry with me."

"Sorry. I'm not angry with you. But look at us — we've been prying into poor Claude's private life, and now we're falling out with Baudouin."

"Yes. You're right."

"I was happy enough to go along with it, but I'll be damned if I'm going to go out of my way to try to find evidence that brave and patriotic men like those two bumped off Grindlethorpe. Like you, I don't think Baudouin did it, but if he did, then frankly I don't much care anymore. So, I'm just going to report back to Ruskin what Baudouin told us. Can I see you home?"

"Walk with me as far as the Metropolitan Line, if you like."

"Yes, if we pick it up at King's Cross, that's near where my digs are. And we need to talk, Eunice. I've made a mistake, a terrible mistake and…"

"Not now, Gus. Not tonight. Let's get this thing out of the way first. Then we can talk for as long as you like."

As they walked from St James's Park towards Piccadilly, Eunice pushed her arm through Gus's. *This time*, he thought, *she isn't acting*.

PART THREE: DECEMBER 1942

CHAPTER 30

It had been a routine moonlight sortie. Gus had flown two Joes into France using the same flak-free channels as usual. Identification of the landing zone had been good, and his landing close to perfect.

There was just one passenger to bring back, an RAF flight crew member smuggled out by the Resistance. One of the French agents on the ground had passed him a briefcase of documents and a bottle of wine. A nice bonus.

"What's your name, mate?"

"Ieuan Jones. I was the flight engineer on a Lancaster. Rest of the crew bought it."

"Sorry to hear that. We'll soon have you home."

The return flight was uneventful until Gus encountered the E-boat. He was flying low over the Channel when he saw it coming towards him. It was an S26, one of the larger boats which had entered service with the Kriegsmarine in 1940. These E-boats, or *Schnellboot* as the Germans called them, were fast torpedo boats capable of thirty-nine knots and armed with two 20mm anti-aircraft guns. It was the guns which worried Gus.

The E-boat must have been heading home after a reconnaissance sortie, he guessed. By the time he saw it, it was too late to gain the necessary height to avoid those light AA guns.

Instinctively he banked to port as the flak opened up. He felt the powerful vibrations as the gunfire ripped into the aeroplane, jolting its frame viciously from side to side. Gus fought to keep control of the Lysander, but nothing was easy when under intense fire.

Then the roar of the engine stopped. It had cut out.

Gus levelled the Lysander as it glided down towards the water's surface. He quickly realised that he was going to have to ditch the kite, and his training kicked in immediately. Without thinking, he opened the cockpit canopy.

This wasn't the first time he'd been forced to ditch his aircraft in the sea. First there had been the Morane-Saulnier in June 1940. He'd taken the aeroplane from a French airfield, intending to fly himself and his gunner, an airman called Morton, home from Dunkirk, but the plane had run out of fuel halfway across the Channel. Gus recalled that as it lost height and approached the water, he had tried to lift its nose with the intention of making a level bellyflop of a landing. It hadn't worked. The left-hand leg of the fixed undercarriage had hit the water first, spinning the plane over to port and pitching both him and Morton into the drink.

Then, in 1941, there had been the Bristol Blenheim that he'd crash-landed off Corfu. At least that kite had had a fully retractable undercarriage. Gus remembered the feeling as the aircraft had slowed and lost height alarmingly. He could still hear the crash of metal on water as the Blenheim had bellyflopped into the Ionian Sea.

It was better to ditch into wind if possible, and if the sea was calm. The wind would slow the Lysander, allowing it to impact the water as slowly as possible and reducing the shock. Gus looked down and saw white horses on the tops of the waves, which ruled out ditching into wind.

The second-best alternative was to ditch along the swell, accepting the crosswind effect and higher speed. This would be preferable to nosing into the face of a wave, which was likely to cause extreme damage to the kite. In addition, Gus knew the Lysander's fixed undercarriage would be a problem, just as the Morane-Saulnier's had been. There would be no chance of a bellyflop. One or other of the wheels would touch the surface first, tossing the Lysander over. He made a snap decision.

"Get your Mae West on, Ieuan. Quick. We're going to bail out before she hits the water."

Gus unstrapped, clambered out and slid onto one of the wing struts as the Lysander glided gently towards the sea. He got his passenger out, then began blowing into the hose to inflate his Mae West. Ieuan followed suit.

He wondered just where they were. Somewhere mid-Channel. He knew the wind was blowing steadily from the west but had no idea what the tidal currents were doing. An ebbing tide might counter the wind and keep them pretty much stationary, but a flood tide, the wind with it, would push the two of them eastward into narrower waters.

The life vest slowly inflated. Ten feet above the water, Gus shouted, "Right, you go first! Now!"

The flight engineer jumped into the water. Gus followed him, going feet-first into the sea. The cold struck them immediately as they watched the Lysander hit the water, lurch to starboard, then tip over onto its top.

Gus knew the water was relatively ambient in the winter because of the Gulf Stream, but that knowledge didn't help. It felt freezing cold.

His life vest was partially inflated, so he blew frantically to get it fully blown-up as the Lysander quickly disappeared. Where were they? Would the E-boat turn back to pick him up so that he might join Duncan in a German POW camp? Surely not, for the sky would soon be illuminated and the skipper of the boat would prefer a cosy berth in Le Havre or Cherbourg than chance being spotted and attacked by RAF fighters.

Gus reached out a hand to the other airman. "Hold on, Ieuan. We need to stay together. Don't let go on any account. Understand?"

"Y-y-yes," he stammered.

"It's useless trying to swim." Gus knew that swimming would expose their limbs and create greater blood flow. The twin effect of this would only serve to accelerate heat loss.

It mattered little that Gus didn't know where they were. His incoming flight path would have been tracked by radar and, hopefully, someone would notice the Lysander's disappearance. They'd report it to RAF Air-Sea Rescue, who would locate them then send out a boat to pick them up. Or so he hoped.

During the Battle of Britian, a pilot downed in the North Sea or English Channel had a twenty per cent chance of being successfully rescued. The RAF insisted the chances were far better now and had informed all their air crews of this. But this was December. The night sky was dark, and the 1932 pattern Mae Wests that they wore were camouflaged. Gus wondered how long they could survive.

He had to be patient, had to wait this out. He and Ieuan needed to keep as warm as possible, to conserve what body heat they still had.

"Hold your right arm against your chest and fold it in front of you. Hold your thighs together. If you can, raise them slightly to protect your groin area."

Gus did the same. This would help to reduce the circulation of cold water all around his body.

After what seemed like an eternity but was actually less than half an hour, Gus heard an aircraft engine. He looked up towards the sound and saw a biplane approaching. It was a Supermarine Walrus.

"Just look at that," he said, waving. They saw the biplane's wings dip, a sign that the pilot had spotted them. The Walrus made a fly-by, turning downwind, then turned again, into wind, slowing down and losing height. As the Walrus flew overhead, something dropped from it. A life raft hit the water about fifty yards upwind of him.

Gus let go of Ieuan and swam towards the inflatable life raft, which floated towards him. He knew he would have just one chance of catching hold of it. As the inflatable came closer, he spotted the ropes which surrounded it, reached out a hand and clutched desperately. Clinging onto the ropes with both hands now, he shouted to Ieuan. Gus swung his left leg up onto one of the buoyancy chambers that ran down each side of the raft. He paused to catch his breath, then, with a final mighty effort, he rolled himself into the life raft.

At first, he just lay on the floor of the inflatable, gasping for breath and shivering. He was alive. He was safe. He looked out for the flight engineer, spotted him and urged him to swim towards the raft. Seconds later he was pulling Ieuan out of the water and into the safety of the life raft.

What to do now? What did the training say?

Gus made sure the floor and buoyancy chambers were fully inflated using the hand pump, then deployed the sea anchor to halt his movement. Next, he bailed out the water and used a sponge provided to dry the inside of the raft. He decided to keep his Mae West on, just in case, then lay on the floor of the raft to shield himself from the wind.

"Hopefully, that Walrus crew will have radioed our position. A rescue boat will be with us soon," he said to Ieuan.

The inflatable raft bobbed around on the moderate sea. Gus felt seasick. Soon, he began vomiting; he knew that his retching would use up valuable energy but was unable to stop. Once there was nothing left in his stomach, he curled up in a foetal position, Ieuan by his side.

"Can you hear something?"

"D-d-don't think so," replied the engineer.

"Listen. I think it's an engine."

"The E-E-E-boat?"

"No. It's a recue craft. Got to be."

As a boat sped towards them, engines screaming, Gus passed out. The next thing he heard was a voice shouting at him. "Come on, mate, reach up!"

He tried to move, but nothing happened. Then slowly he raised his right arm and a crewman grabbed it. Ieuan was pushing him upwards. Another man took hold of his Mae West straps, and between them they hauled Gus from the life raft and into the boat. He sat there, shivering and looking around as the crew pulled up the flight engineer. He recognised the boat as a Type Two RAF 'Whaleback', a high-speed launch that was powered by three Napier Sea Lion engines.

The medical orderly and another crew member got Gus and Ieuan inside and helped them to remove their wet clothing. Then they wrapped them in woollen blankets and placed woollen balaclavas over their heads. Someone brought Gus a mug of sweetened tea and encouraged him to chew a chocolate bar.

"I've n-not seen one of these for y-years," he said, his lips numb from the cold.

"We try to keep a few on board. Get them from the Yanks," said the medical orderly. "How are you feeling?"

"N-not too bad, thanks," said Gus. "C-cold."

"Don't you worry. You'll soon warm up now. We'll be back in Weymouth before you know it. Forgive me for boring you two with my chatter, but I don't want you to fall asleep. You mustn't doze off. Got it?"

"G-got it, yes."

They'd warmed up by the time the Whaleback pulled into Weymouth harbour. The crew got them ashore and took them to a shoreside building where a fire was burning, mugs of tea were waiting for them and the smell of a cooked breakfast issued from a kitchen to the rear.

"We'll get your clothes dried out," said a civilian. "Then you can look all respectable again, ready for your journey home."

"Home," said Ieuan. "Now, that would be something."

CHAPTER 31

Eunice and Ruskin had come to visit Gus in RAF Hospital Wroughton, which was in Wiltshire. Ruskin sat in a chair beside the hospital bed, whilst Eunice perched on the edge of the bed itself.

"How are you, young man?"

"I'm all right, thanks, Guv. A few more days and I'll be out of here."

"That's good news."

"They say you nearly died out there, Gus."

"They're exaggerating. I got a bit too cold, that's all. As I say, I'll be out of here soon. I need to be. The food is bloody dreadful."

Luckily, Gus was in a private ward which provided the anonymity they needed, so Ruskin jumped in with the important question. "You're sure you're up to discussing the investigation?"

"Yes. But you'll need to talk me through everything, if you don't mind. Just to be sure I haven't lost my memory," said Gus.

"I'll do that," said Eunice, taking a deep breath. "Titus Grindlethorpe's killing wasn't random. It wasn't done by a robber or another petty criminal. He was murdered for a reason. Most probably something to do with Operation Lodz or the Dieppe report..."

"Or because Peacock thought he was taking dirty money from somewhere," said Gus.

"Was he? Are we sure of that?" asked Ruskin.

"Peacock was right about the money in one sense. There was no way Grindlethorpe could afford to live where he did on a squadron leader's salary. But we can't be sure it was dirty money — a pay-off for undercover work or spying."

"You're right," said Eunice, "but it doesn't really matter. Let's return to what we know. Grindlethorpe believed he was being followed. He suspected a number of people, so let's go through them. First, me — outrageous suggestion, and I have an alibi. Second, Duncan Farquhar, but he's in a German POW camp."

"Third, me, of course," said Gus.

"You have a motive and no alibi, but we know it wasn't you. Fourth, Krawiec. He has a motive, Lodz, but he also has an alibi; he was away in Canada. So does Peacock; he's fifth on the list of suspects. His motive is the Dieppe report or the dirty money, but Peacock was ill at home, confined to his bed. He has two people who can back it up. That leaves suspect six, Baudouin, and suspect seven, Claude, as possibilities. Both had a motive, the Dieppe report, and the opportunity, and neither has an alibi."

"It isn't either of them," said Gus. "I'm convinced of it. I'm sure we can rule them out. Neither has an alibi, I agree, but neither do they have a strong motive. Neither of them actually knew Grindlethorpe. They've only heard Eunice and me talking about him. It just doesn't feel right."

"Then we've ruled out everyone on Grindlethorpe's list," said Eunice.

"Hold on a minute," said Gus. "A man like Peacock wouldn't have had to do the killing himself; he could have arranged for someone else to do it for him."

"While ensuring he had an alibi," added Ruskin, coughing again.

"That's a good point," said Eunice. "We've assumed all along that it was the person with the motive who followed Grindlethorpe and then murdered him. But what if it was someone acting on Peacock's orders?"

"Does he have that kind of power?" asked Ruskin.

"Probably," said Eunice.

"So does Krawiec," added Gus. "He has a bunch of thugs working for him on special ops. They wouldn't hesitate."

"Which of them is most likely to know someone ruthless enough to carry out a killing on the streets of London?"

"Krawiec," said Gus. "He's in charge of a team of unscrupulous killers. It would be pretty easy for him to organise. He could have just ordered Grindlethorpe's death. He wouldn't have needed to give a reason."

"But let's not lose track of Peacock. Could he have ordered it?"

"No," said Gus. "That would be totally out of his remit. I suppose he might have been able to twist the arm of someone who owed him a favour, but it would have been much harder for Peacock to have Grindlethorpe bumped off. My money is still on Krawiec."

"Wait a minute," said Eunice. "What if those two were in it together? Both have good reasons for wanting Grindlethorpe out of the way. So, let's assume they both arranged alibis and Krawiec got one of his SOE men to do the dirty work. But they knew that sooner or later a Metropolitan Police detective would get near the truth, so Peacock used his influence to get you, Guv, taken off the case and replaced by Flight Lieutenant Colson of the Royal Air Force Police, Special Investigation Branch. Then Peacock leaned on Colson and told him to stop the investigation, or at least put it on ice."

"Yes," said Ruskin, "that fits together nicely, doesn't it? I can see how that would work."

"We can't prove it, though, can we?" said Eunice.

Ruskin sighed. "No, Peacock and Krawiec both have alibis, and there's no way we could ever track down the SOE chappie that wielded the blow. If one did."

"Which — if he did — he was doing under orders, motivated by patriotism and fraternity," said Gus.

"So, it ends here, does it?" asked Eunice.

"Yes, I think it does," said Gus, looking at Ruskin, who shook his head slowly.

"No. I just can't let a murder on my patch go unsolved. I agree that as far as you two are concerned, this is the end of the matter. But I'm going to get to the truth. It's either Krawiec or Peacock. Or, as you suggest, the two of them in it together. I'm going to find out."

"Be careful, Guv. You could get yourself into big trouble."

"He's right, Guv. You've a lot to lose."

"As it happens, you're both wrong. You see, I'm finishing work this week. Signed off on grounds of ill health. It's cancer. My doctor thinks I've only got a couple of months to live. So I've got nothing to lose, have I?"

"Oh no, Guv! I'm so sorry."

"No need to be. My own fault, really. Too many smokes. Far too many."

"If you're going to carry on with the investigation, you can count me in, too," said Gus.

"No!" insisted Eunice. "You can't possibly, but I can. What have you got in mind, Guv?"

"We've overlooked a possible source of evidence: the bobby on the beat around Regent's Park the night Grindlethorpe was killed. He didn't find the body, so he hasn't been interviewed.

I'd have got to him, of course, if the Met hadn't been taken off the case."

"And you think he may have noticed something?"

"Nothing obvious, no. Nothing directly linked to a murder. He'd have volunteered the information straight away if that were the case. But now we have a lead on who might be responsible. Just a chat might throw up something. And I don't need either of you with me for that. I can let Eunice know if I find out anything, and she can tell you, Gus. That's my final word."

"All right, Governor," said Gus. "Fine with me."

After his visitors had left, Gus went to the hospital canteen to eat alongside some of the other recuperating officers. He wondered if Ruskin would uncover any new leads, but wasn't sure he cared that much. Grindlethorpe hadn't been any great loss to the SOE or to the war effort in general. He'd be easy to replace. Maybe it would be better to let sleeping dogs lie.

He understood Ruskin's frustration. Leaving the police force on medical grounds with an unsolved murder case behind him must have been difficult. But it wasn't his fault, and no one could possibly hold it against him.

Gus slept well that night. In fact, since his spell in the Channel and the subsequent hypothermia, he'd been sleeping much better. He'd not needed to take his phenobarbital tablets for days. Perhaps he was cured of the damned insomnia, he thought, swapping one illness for another. But he didn't feel ill. He felt surprisingly well. He felt like getting back to work, back to flying, back to fighting the war.

He'd heard it was beginning to turn in favour of the Allies. In November, news had emerged of the German army in full retreat in North Africa, after suffering a battering at El

Alamein. Operation Torch, the Allied invasion of North Africa, had begun with troops landing near Casablanca, Oran and Algiers. The December news was that, following weeks of heavy fighting on the Eastern Front, the Red Army had launched an attack that encircled the Germans at Stalingrad.

Whether this was worth all the death and destruction was another matter, but yes, he thought, the Allies had reason to be hopeful. It was time for Gus to get back to RAF Tempsford.

CHAPTER 32

"Fancy taking a Hudson up for a spin tomorrow?" asked Doggie Russell, the day after Gus had returned to Tempsford.

"Why? Do you have one that needs a test flight? Like the Lizzie that cut out on me a few weeks ago?"

"No, but we need somebody to fly King George down to Plymouth."

"The king? Are you serious?"

"Absolutely serious, old boy. Mouse — I mean, Wing Commander Fielden — is otherwise engaged, and the flight leader has a broken hand. We can't very well have a junior pilot fly His Majesty around, can we? You're the next most senior officer available that's been cleared to fly Lockheed Hudsons. I'm afraid it just has to be you, Bouncer."

"I don't know. I've been back with the squadron for less than two months. In that time, I've had to emergency land a duff Lizzie and ditch another in the drink. Now, one day after I've been declared fit for normal duties, I get a date with the king. I'll make this my first and last drink," said Gus, sipping his Whisky Mac. "I certainly don't want to have a thick head tomorrow."

The next morning, after a decent breakfast of bacon and eggs, Gus flew the Hudson down to RAF Hendon in north London. It was an armed version of the aeroplane, and a flight sergeant called Bowers was manning the gun turret. The only other crew member aboard was a sergeant called Wicker, who was observer and flight engineer.

Most importantly, however, Wicker was a steward and would be serving drinks in the reasonably comfortable cabin the king would use.

Gus gazed down from the cockpit. King George walked across the apron dressed in the uniform of an admiral. *He must be going to Plymouth to inspect some ships*, thought Gus. Or perhaps he would visit the Royal Naval Hospital. He was accompanied by a senior naval officer and an Air Vice-Marshal that Gus didn't recognise.

The flight from London to RAF Roborough on the northern edge of Plymouth was just under an hour. Gus had a route that took him west to South Wales, south to the northern mass of Dartmoor and then on an approach from Exeter, westward into wind, to Roborough.

When they were over Bristol, Wicker came into the cockpit. "Pardon me, sir, but the king is asking who the pilot is and saying he would like to come up front, if he may," he said.

"What? Is that usual?"

"No idea, sir, but unless you feel it's unsafe, I don't see how we can turn him down, do you?"

"No. No, it's fine, Wicker. Bring him up."

"Right away, sir."

"Oh, Wicker, how should I address him?"

"'Your Majesty' is the correct way to address him in the first instance, sir. After that, it's 'sir'."

Minutes later, Gus was pointing out places of interest to King George VI, who was at his right-hand side. The Air Vice-Marshal had also poked his head into the cockpit.

"W-w-we do have an escort today, do we?" asked the king, with his familiar stutter.

"Yes, Your Majesty," said Gus. "There's a flight of Spitfires up above us, keeping a look out. You can't see them, sir, but they've been coming in and out over the radio."

"G-g-good. Well, thank you for your careful pilotage, er..."

"Flight Lieutenant Beaumont, sir."

"Thank you, F-f-flight Lieutenant."

"We're about to turn to port, sir, then I will begin preparation for landing. Best that you go back and strap in, sir, if you wouldn't mind."

"Y-y-yes, of course," said King George. And with that, he returned to the cabin.

Gus had orders to depart Roborough as soon as the king had been delivered, as His Majesty would stay in Plymouth overnight before recommencing his royal duties the following day. Presumably, another pilot — Fielden, perhaps — would bring him back later.

Gus was free to choose the route back and, unlike on the outward journey, there would be no flight of Spitfires to keep a watchful eye on the Hudson. Not that it was a problem; the Luftwaffe hadn't been active over southern England for many months, except for those damned Jabo tip-and-run raids, which had caused terror and panic all over the south coast.

Rather than taking a direct, north-easterly route to Tempsford, Gus decided he would fly east, clinging to the coast until he got over Worthing, then turn north. He informed Bowers and Wicker, instructing them to keep a watchful eye over the skies to be on the safe side.

They'd just cleared the Isle of Wight when a voice came over the RT.

"Bandits, bandits!" shouted Bowers.

"Where are they, Bowers?" Gus demanded.

"One o'clock and very low, out to sea. See them, Skipper?"

Gus scanned the sky. There they were. Two small aircraft, and he could just make out black crosses on the wings. Focke-Wulf 190s, most likely. "I see them, Sergeant. Get the guns ready, just in case."

Gus knew the Fw-190s, Jabo fighter bombers, had no interest in the Hudson. Each of them was armed with a bomb, and they were going to wreak as much havoc and destruction as they could manage. But not if he could stop them.

Gus had seen Fw-190 Jabos in action before. Their tactic was to fly very low, almost at wavetop level, over the Channel to avoid radar. Once they were about a mile or so off the target, they would climb to five hundred feet, then dive steeply and release their bombs directly over the target.

As he looked at the Jabos, the first of them began to climb, followed by the second.

The Jabos were now almost immediately to the right of the Hudson. Bower's machine guns would be useless against these fast fighter-bombers, but Gus had an idea. Quickly he turned to starboard and descended to five hundred feet. Within seconds, the Hudson was at the same height as the leading Jabo and was heading straight towards it.

"Brace, brace," said Gus over the RT.

"Crikey, Skipper!" shouted Wicker, who was just behind Gus. "We're going to hit the bugger! You'll get us all killed."

"Hopefully not," said Gus, "but get to the back of the aircraft and brace yourself. Quick as you can, Sergeant."

It was a game of chicken. Who would pull out first, Gus or the Luftwaffe pilot? As the gap quickly closed, Gus shouted over the RT, "I'm going to go under the bloody thing! Bowers, you might get a chance to have a shot at one or the other of them. Ready?"

"Ready, Skipper."

Gus pushed the stick forward. The nose of the Hudson dipped, making him lose sight of the oncoming German planes. Then he pulled up. Nothing directly ahead. He heard the sound of the Brownings coming from behind him.

"I hit the wingman, Skipper," said Bowers. "He's smoking and pulling to our right."

"Good shooting, Bowers. But keep a lookout — his mate may well be after us."

Gus put himself in the position of a German Jabo pilot who'd just been shot at by a lone, sluggish and lightly armed twin-engined aeroplane. The Jabo's guns were armed, ready for ground-strafing. The pilot would ditch the bomb and come after the Hudson.

Gus turned to port and put the Hudson into a one hundred and eighty-degree turn. North — away from the coast, away from the Channel and, crucially, away from the Jabos' home base in France. Then he descended to treetop level.

"He can only attack us from above, so keep your eyes peeled, both of you," Gus ordered. He then radioed for help. RAF Tangmere was close by and, hopefully, once they picked up his call, they would scramble a flight of Spitfires or Hurricanes to fight off the Focke-Wulfs.

"They're going home," said Bowers. "I can see them. One smoking badly, the other watching his tail. They're not interested in us and haven't hit anything below us. Good work, Skipper."

Good work? Putting the lives of his crew, the aircraft and himself at risk — was that good work? It was instinct, that was all. Gus hadn't thought about it; he'd just done it. *Oh God*, he thought. What if King George had still been on board? Would he have done the same thing? He didn't want to consider where his instincts could lead him.

CHAPTER 33

Eunice had arranged to meet Gus in London on the Saturday of his weekend leave. She chose the pub in South Kensington and told him to be there as soon after six p.m. as he could.

The pub was bustling as he went inside. He looked around for Eunice but couldn't spot her, so he bought himself a drink and waited.

When she arrived, he thought she looked flustered. She saw him, waved and walked over to where he was sitting.

"Drink?"

"Let me tell you something first."

"Go ahead."

"DI Ruskin isn't well at all. Days to go, I think. Maybe not even that. But he's found something."

"Tell me. Start at the beginning."

"He managed to track down the policemen that were patrolling the Regent's Park beat on the night of the murder. There are three. He spoke to two of them. The first bobby, PC Close, had little to contribute, but he did see something slightly odd on the last late shift he completed before Grindlethorpe's death. Three nights before. It wasn't suspicious in itself, but knowing what we know now, Ruskin thought it important.

"On one of the streets just off Marylebone Road, PC Close spotted a man lingering in a doorway. He was a thick-set, heavily built man in his twenties, dressed in dark clothing. Close approached him and asked the man what he was doing there. He said he was waiting for a friend and asked the policeman if he had a light for his cigarette. Of course, the bobby couldn't help. The interesting thing from Ruskin's point of view was that this stranger spoke in a heavy Eastern European accent."

"Polish?"

"Could have been."

"Was it followed up at all?"

"No. PC Close didn't think it was important."

"On its own, it isn't," said Gus. "You said he spoke to two police officers?"

"Yes. The second was PC Stokes. He was on lates the night Grindlethorpe was killed. He spotted a man fitting the same description coming away from the site of Grindlethorpe's murder, heading towards Marylebone station."

"Did the officer speak to him?"

"Yes. Stokes asked him if he was lost."

"And?"

"The man asked the way to Marylebone station, even though he was heading straight for it."

"He may have been confused in the blackout. Disorientated."

"Perhaps, but PC Stokes said the man spoke with a Polish accent."

"How could he be so sure?"

"PC Stokes lives in Ealing. His neighbours are Polish immigrants. He told Ruskin that he's confident he can recognise the accent. He's one hundred per cent sure the man he saw was Polish."

"Are you thinking what I'm thinking, Eunice?"

"This points very firmly to Krawiec."

"Yes," agreed Gus. "What does Ruskin think?"

"He thinks the man spotted by PC Close and PC Stokes was probably one and the same — one of Krawiec's SOE thugs." Eunice paused. "But I still think Krawiec and Peacock acted together. It makes sense. Peacock suspected Grindlethorpe of concealing the Dieppe report and had noticed there was something amiss regarding his personal wealth. Krawiec suspected him of betraying Operation Lodz. They conspired to have Grindlethorpe killed, making sure that they themselves had alibis. Then, they got Baudouin and Claude to do it…"

"What?" Gus exclaimed.

"Oh, don't you see? It's exactly like *Murder on the Orient Express*. They all had a hand in it, Gus." She gave a wry smile.

"Yes," he said, "and I suppose those two, Baudouin and Claude, have simply excellent Polish accents when they need them. They wouldn't question orders, either." He sighed. "You say Ruskin's very ill? Close to the end?"

"Yes."

"Will he take this any further?"

"He can't, Gus. He's dying."

"Then we leave it be. If Krawiec and Peacock have got away with anything, it's with eliminating a man who at least was a thorn in everyone's side and, at worst, was a traitor. I know I've said this before, but the world is no worse off with Grindlethorpe dead."

Eunice nodded. "You're right. Better that we forget the whole thing. Please may I have that drink now?"

"What can I get you?"

"A G and T would be nice, thanks."

Gus made his way to the bar. Eventually he caught the barmaid's eye and ordered a pint of bitter for himself and a gin and tonic for Eunice. As he walked back to their table, Gus decided now was the time to seize the bull by the horns, so to speak.

He sat down, placing the drinks on the table. "Can we talk? Please? There's something I've been trying to say for a few weeks now."

Eunice looked at him. "What have you to say, Gus?"

"That I've made a horrible, terrible mistake and I'm dreadfully sorry about it."

She remained silent.

"It was the state of my mind, you see," Gus went on. "I think I've been under the cosh for months. I wasn't able to sleep. I began making mistakes because I was so bloody tired. Then I was suspected of murder, and there was that awful news about Butch Paderewski on top of everything else." He shook his head slowly, a tear running down his cheek. "The work those bomber crews undertake is horrific, Eunice. I don't know how they cope."

"I'm sure you've seen horrible things, Gus."

"Yes, I have. But that's not what I mean. It's the bombing of innocent civilians. The destruction of towns and cities. I tried to raise it in the mess at Elvington. That didn't go down too well. Few wanted to face up to it. I think I made myself unpopular there."

"I can understand that."

Gus wiped his eyes. "Then I came back from a particularly messy bombing raid. I can't go into details, but it really was awful. I think it altered my sense of right and wrong. I became totally unbalanced. When I wrote you that letter and called off our engagement, I didn't know what I was doing. It was a mistake, the worst mistake of my life. Please say that you'll forgive me, Eunice. Please say that we can carry on as we were, that you'll marry me. Will you?"

"Did you find somebody else? In your letter, you said you'd found another lover."

"No, of course not. Well, I mean, I didn't fall in love with someone else, if that's what you're asking. I just said that to make it easier on myself, so that I didn't have to explain. There was a woman — a WAAF. Izzy, she was called. I'm so sorry, Eunice."

Gus looked into her eyes. She picked up her glass, drained it, and placed it back down.

"Could you get me another drink, please, Gus?"

"Yes, of course. What would you like? Same again?"

"What I'd really like is a lovely Kir Royale, but I suppose I could settle for a gin and tonic. We've got some serious talking to do, you and I. We have a wedding to plan, if you recall."

Gus smiled and nodded, relieved.

"And," Eunice went on, pausing to take something from her handbag, "perhaps I can start wearing this again."

Gus looked at the engagement ring. The emerald and diamonds sparkled as they caught the light. He sighed with gratitude. "Yes, darling," he said. "That would be simply perfect." He gently pushed the ring onto her finger.

HISTORICAL NOTES

CHARACTERS AND PERSONALITIES

Wing Commander Sir Alexander Peacock is entirely fictitious, though I expect military types like him were scattered all over wartime London. Peacock recruits Gus Beaumont for service in the Special Operations Executive (SOE). The SOE was formed in 1940 from the amalgamation of three existing secret organisations (MI6, the Electra House Department, and MI(R), the guerrilla warfare research department of the War Office). The purpose of the SOE was to conduct reconnaissance, espionage and sabotage against the Axis powers in occupied Europe, and to aid local resistance movements.

Air Marshal Arthur Harris was nicknamed Butch (short for Butcher) by RAF bomber crews. This was not, however, a reflection on any disregard for civilian casualties of the bombing raids. It was a comment on the high losses amongst the bomber crews themselves.

The story of Butch Paderewski's death is based on the case of Lieutenant James Smith RFA. Lieutenant Smith, who had served throughout the First World War and had been diagnosed with neurasthenia/shellshock, died after being hit by a train near Exeter in May 1920. The inquest recorded an open verdict.

Wing Commander (later Group Captain, then Air Commodore) Edward Hedley 'Mouse' Fielden was, at various times during the war, King George VI's personal pilot, CO of 161 Squadron and Station Commander of RAF Tempsford.

Gordon Cummins, the Blackout Killer, murdered four women and attempted to murder two others in London over a six-day period in February 1942. He was convicted in April and hanged at Wandsworth Prison in June that year.

PLACES

Audley End House in Essex was used as a general holding camp for the SOE, eventually becoming the base of a Polish branch. The Polish SOE War Memorial in the main drive commemorates one hundred and five Polish SOE personnel who died in World War Two.

RAF Davidstow Moor is located near Camelford in North Cornwall. It was used by the RAF from late 1942 until 1945 but was one of Coastal Command's lesser used airfields. It is now the home of a very interesting, if eclectic collection of aviation/military artifacts and the Davidstow creamery. The squash court is still intact.

What was once Fort Lamy in French Equatorial Africa is now N'Djamena, the capital of Chad.

Camp X was the unofficial name of the secret SOE training school 103, located on the shore of Lake Ontario, Canada.

AIRCRAFT

The cover illustration shows a Short Stirling bomber flying over the German city of Lübeck. Though most Stirlings were used in night bombing raids, on 16th July 1942 the Stirlings of 218 Squadron were involved in a daylight raid on the Lübecker Flender Werke AG (a U-boat assembly plant) in Lübeck.

Soon after the outbreak of war, the King's Flight was equipped with an armed Lockheed Hudson, an aircraft developed from an airliner. Later, in 1942, the role of transporting the Royal Family was transferred to 161 Squadron.

Creep-back was the tendency of bombers using optical bombsights to release their load before time, leading to a gradual spread backwards along the attack vector away from the intended target.

SQUADRONS

77 Squadron was based at RAF Elvington from October 1942 to May 1944. It lost 82 aircraft and 450 aircrew while based there.

Thiès Squadron is fictitious. I based it on the two French squadrons, 346 'Guyenne' and 347 'Tunisie', which moved to RAF Elvington much later in the war (May 1944) than the French squadron in this novel. Squadrons (escadrilles) of the Free French Air Force were named after French provinces, for example the Escadrille Normandie, which served with the Soviets on the Eastern Front. Elvington was the only airfield in the United Kingdom used by the Free French Forces. It is now a museum, and one of the remaining Nissen huts there is presented as the French officers' mess.

A French Groupe de Bombardement (bombers) or Groupe de Chasse (fighters) was equivalent to an RAF Wing, around three squadrons.

MISSIONS AND OPERATIONS

There has been much debate over the merits or otherwise of Operation Jubilee, the Dieppe Raid (which is the backcloth to *Bouncer's Butcherbird*). A good overview of the background and execution of Operation Jubilee from one who considers the operation to be a disaster can be found in Patrick Bishop's *Operation Jubilee, Dieppe 1942: The Folly and the Sacrifice* (Penguin, 1997).

Lodz is a fictious operation, fully detailed in book three of this series, *Bouncer's Butcherbird*. It is loosely based on Jeffrey Bines' account of the real Operation Freston.

Fleets of unprotected Boeing B-17 Flying Fortresses of the US Eighth Air Force began to fly daylight raids against the German industrial heartland in late January 1943. In this novel, I have them begin two months earlier.

OTHER

GEE was a hyperbolic radio-navigation system. It worked by measuring the time delay between two radio signals to produce a navigational fix. Adopted by RAF Bomber Command in 1942, GEE was accurate to a few hundred yards at ranges up to three hundred and fifty miles.

Mae West was the nickname adopted by RAF air crews for their inflatable life vests. These were named after Mae West, a popular actress, singer and comedian based in the USA.

The RAF Marine Craft Section was formed in 1918 with the explicit purpose of rescuing pilots and aircrew from the sea. Apart from the humanitarian case for rescue, air crew were regarded as scarce commodities during the war. From 1941, air-sea rescue functioned under the Directorate of Air-Sea Rescue, whose motto was "the sea shall not have them". They operated both aircraft and boats, such as the sixty-three-foot-long Type 2 High Speed Launch, the 'Whaleback', which was capable of thirty-six knots.

In 1942, a sophisticated nationwide counterfeiting ring stood trial, but most forgeries of ration books and clothing coupons proved to be untraceable.

A NOTE TO THE READER

Dear Reader.

Thank you for taking the time to read *Bouncer's Bomber*. I hope you enjoyed reading it as much as I enjoyed writing it.

Reviews are invaluable to authors, so if you liked the book, I'd be grateful if you could leave a review on **Amazon** or **Goodreads**.

Readers can connect with me online **on Facebook** and **X (formerly Twitter)**.

I hope we meet again in Gus Beaumont's next adventure!

Tony Rea

Sapere Books is an exciting new publisher of brilliant fiction and popular history.

To find out more about our latest releases and our monthly bargain books visit our website:
saperebooks.com

www.ingramcontent.com/pod-product-compliance
Lightning Source LLC
Chambersburg PA
CBHW020604180626
46810CB00007B/2647